Irenosen Okojie is a Nigerian British writer. Her debut novel *Butterfly Fish* won a Betty Trask award and was shortlisted for an Edinburgh International First Book Award. Her work has been featured in the *New York Times*, *Observer*, *Guardian*, the BBC and the Huffington Post amongst other publications. Her short story collection *Speak Gigantular*, published by Jacaranda Books, was shortlisted for the Edgehill Short Story Prize, the Jhalak Prize, the Saboteur Awards and nominated for a Shirley Jackson Award. She was recently inducted as a fellow of the Royal Society of Literature as one of the Forty Under Forty initiative.

'Weird and wild ... An extraordinary collection of surreal tales' *Guardian*

'Irenosen Okojie is one of our finest short story writers. *Nudibranch* is her second collection and in it her imagination runs riot. Linguistically inventive and always unpredictable, there is an emotional intensity and weirdness to her story telling that haunts and lingers' Bernardine Evaristo, *Observer* Best Books of 2019

'There are few writers who possess quite the boundless daring of Irenosen Okojie, whose second collection of short stories, *Nudibranch*, is dazzling, a feast for the senses, as well as a lesson in both creative and existential bravery' Diana Evans, *Observer* Best Books of 2019

'Okojie writes immersive prose you can get lost in, lulling you into a false sense of security only to turn everything upside down within the space of a sentence ... Disjointed, disorientating and unpredictable but in all the best ways, *Nudibranch* will leave you eager for more at every turn' *The Skinny*

'A theme drifts through these strange stories like a ghost; the search, often thwarted for ~ ̄   ̄tity, a place of safet   ̄er lyrical writing come together [and] her fantastical, disjointed tales speak for our damaged, out-of-kilter times. They are, to borrow her phrase, full of warped, rhapsodic song' *New Internationalist*

'Okojie's imagination is frequently funny, and defiantly weird. Her slippery stories are not bound by logic, time or place; both within and between tales she dives between the genres of fable, dystopia, allegory, lyrically conceived realism, and horror' *The Arts Desk*

'Okojie's latest collection is perfect for those of us who love a weird, moody story that settles in the body and doesn't move on quickly. Reminiscent of Helen Oyeyemi's *What is Not Yours is Not Yours*, with characters ranging from sea goddesses and a time-traveling homeless man to monks that skip between dimensions and appropriately creepy children of the future, these stories are as tightly woven as that blanket you find yourself under while reading. You'll need a flashlight with long battery life, because the prose is so fierce and melodic that you'll be up all night' *Literary Hub*

'Dark and lyrical' *Stylist*

'Surprising, seductive and often heartfelt, this is an entertaining selection that establishes Okojie as one of the country's most impressive writers' *PRIDE*

'There's an irresistible lure to these disparate, experimental works reminiscent of Carmen Maria Machado, Kristen Roupenian or the gothic magic of Isabel Allende. This is writing at its most vital: poignant, performative and disturbing' *Financial Times*

'An extraordinary and unforgettable collection from one of the finest literary imaginations working today' Max Porter

IRENOSEN
OKOJIE

NUDI
BRANCH

dialogue
books

DIALOGUE BOOKS

First published in Great Britain in 2019 by Dialogue Books
This paperback edition published in 2020 by Dialogue Books

10 9 8 7 6 5 4 3 2 1

A CIP catalogue record for this book is available from the British Library.

ISBN 978-0-349-70091-5

Typeset in Berling by M Rules
Printed and bound in Great Britain by Clays Ltd, Elcograf S.p.A.

Papers used by Dialogue Books are from well-managed forests
and other responsible sources.

MIX
Paper from
responsible sources
FSC® C104740
www.fsc.org

Dialogue Books
An imprint of
Little, Brown Book Group
Carmelite House
50 Victoria Embankment
London EC4Y 0DZ

An Hachette UK Company
www.hachette.co.uk

www.littlebrown.co.uk

To Mum, Dad, Amen, Ota and Iredia,
so much love always.

To women whose reconfigurations in the
dark become embers by dawn.

CONTENTS

Logarithm

Here is a skillet. Here is a loaf of rye bread. Here is a river. Here are two reflections for it. Here is a chintz skirt. Here is a rib on a bend. Here is a dawn carrying December. Here is a memory growing tentacles in a tall, grainy jar. Here is the umbilical cord slung over the rose-coloured lampshade. Here are the reins for figures that become injuries. Here are two wrists marked with soot. Here is a table. Here are its legs. Here is the shape that departed. Here is the wood. Here is the canvas. Here is the atom. Here is the collision. Here is the infant's dummy. Here is the blade. Here is the mirror. Here is the right-angle. Here is the cut. Here is the pulp. Here is the runny cherimoya. Here is the cassava. Here is the yam. Here is the pulse. Here is the defect. Here is the smoke. Here is the jackal food rising beneath the tablecloth. Here is the spill. Here is the magician. Here is the pocket. Here is the trick. Here is the light bulb. Here is the wattage. Here is the logo. Here are your fingerprints as hostages. Here is the vow. Here is the burial soil. Here is the margin marrying the peak. Here is the white lie fit for a vein. Here is the graveyard slab. Here is the trampoline. Here is the leaking valve. Here is the golden cup. Here is the net over a dune. Here is the aubergine. Here is the wire. Here is the Dalmatian's limp. Here is the stained bed sheet. Here is the protractor. Here is Jupiter. Here is the circumference created from a haemorrhage. Here is the leap. Here is the dive. Here is the brink crumbling in the gut. Here is the cold hollow. Here is the constellation. Here is the breath. Here is the bark. Here is the body twisting in brine. Here is the wine. Here is the one-way sign in the bath tub. Here is the sweet mist from a clitoris. Here is a throbbing in the ditch. Here are the crinkled leaves you wore to the birth. Here is a crease. Here is a murmur. Here is the riverbank. Here is the currency. Here is the bottled mutation. Here is the edible wheel.

But where is the baby?

Here is there.

Now, what do I do with the woman holding the reins, shrinking from reflections, the nub of a dummy? Licking Eve's rib?

Kookaburra Sweet

Several factors contributed to Kara's series of self-collisions. Several pale, pin-pricked airbags shrank between two victims each time: herself and herself. The airbags wouldn't have been necessary if she hadn't missed her original flight at Sydney airport because her mobile died, which meant no alarm to wake her up. If there hadn't been an issue settling her hostel bill, since the front-desk clerk claimed there was a problem with her Barclaycard, which meant pretending to enter one of the empty pool rooms to call Barclays but slipping into the toilets instead. Then through the window without injuring her legs or alarming the few street kids passing on skateboards, chatting and smoking in clusters.

She jumped out into parched Sydney streets that had become concrete enemies, exiting into the blazing heat, wonky small silver suitcase in tow, wheels squeaking like a distorted instrument for the unlucky. A suitcase full of broken Sydney dreams folded mockingly between bright clothes, her black bartending uniform. And she rushing through traffic to hail a cab, cast out from a bloodshot vision, like a split thirteenth apostle sewn back together.

By the time she reached the airport, made it to the check-in area, breathing heavily as though about to birth something tiny and unrecognisable through her mouth, an offering to the gaunt-faced flight attendant in exchange for good news, it felt too late. The attendant sported a tight brunette bun that made her look severe. Her name badge read 'Christina'. Calmly she said, 'I'm afraid you've missed your flight, love. It left ten minutes ago. You'll have to book another one. You don't have any insurance. There's nothing else I can do.' It was delivered unsympathetically, coldly. Kara got the impression she'd said this many times before in autopilot mode.

She ran a hand through her shoulder-length braids, felt her armpits producing sweat beads to water unfulfilled half-formed women that grew on runways. Bodies swirled around her, flashes of colour on a broad never-ending canvas of travellers, who would drink from the periphery while their fingers moulded plane-engine noise into surprising shapes. The din of the airport rose in the afternoon heat. Her pretty face crumpled. Her heart sank. Her mouth went dry. This was the problem with being late often. It actually changed outcomes when it mattered.

She booked another flight to London, which left her with only a hundred pounds for the rest of the month. *Jesus*

Pontius Pilate Christ! She'd have to eat Rice Krispies for breakfast and lunch and scrambled eggs with sardines and hard-dough bread for dinner for at least two weeks. *Pontius ras clat Pilate.* Kara wandered through the airport shops thinking of home in Forest Hill: the wooden floors, the high white ceilings and large windows.

The stumpy cactus on her cracked kitchen window sill she'd bled on after cutting her finger while slicing plantain. She was convinced it was dead, that her bulbs of blood had sated it only temporarily. She had a way of killing things unwittingly. She pictured the shrivelled cactus, its thirsty soil, the desires she'd hoped would come to fruition in Sydney wearing dead, prickly cactus skin, sitting still on plane seats to be flown to various destinations. She thought of women who didn't know what to do with the sea inside them. Who didn't know how to let it line their paths or flush out neon signs forming in the blood to misdirect them in gloriously foreign countries.

After wandering around for about an hour, she settled into the seating area opposite an Espresso coffee house. She looked up at the screen for an update on her flight. The man to her right watched her curiously. He was Aborigine, dressed in blue jeans, a warm-coloured Aztec-style shirt and a black cowboy hat. His long hair curled past his shoulders. He held a dark brown leather bag. He smiled warmly at her. His broad features stretched. It was a beautiful, welcoming smile. He offered her his hand, shook hers enthusiastically. 'You look like you could do with some good fortune, eh? I'm Kizzy.'

She adjusted herself in her seat, pulling her shoulders up so she didn't slouch. 'Kara. Probably not the best company right now, spent more money today than I have in the last month,' she grumbled.

He chuckled, in a way that was infectious not rude. Not as if he was laughing at her misfortune. 'A good distraction is to talk to a stranger and eat sweets.' His eyes were alert, persuasive, the gold in them darkening intermittently.

'That's your solution to my problems?' she retorted, unconvinced, stretching long, restless legs.

'Well, it's one solution, eh, missy?' His lips curled. He opened his leather bag. Sure enough, it was chock-full of sweets, bright red packets of liquorice begging to be ripped open. The brand name was Kookaburra. Kookaburra liquorice.

'Help yourself,' he instructed. An announcement for an abandoned dog was made on the tannoy. He opened a packet, popped a short stick of liquorice into his mouth, chewing slowly, savouring the taste.

Kara grabbed a handful she'd save for later, stuffing them into her rucksack, like a magician stowing tricks she'd use in time.

Kizzy smelt like spicy incense. His dark, velvety brown skin glowed. Kara imagined the pulse in his neck had a silvery wing flickering beside it, as if it, too, had attempted a flight journey that had gone wrong. A leather watch in his pocket matched his bag, showing the incorrect time of 11 a.m. He began to hum then. A quiet rumbling that got into her bones slowly, a drug transported through song. She didn't think to ask how he'd known she'd suffered a misfortune because the air was charged with something indefinable, molten, till she heard the wing beside his pulse changing direction.

'What does the song mean?' she asked, resisting the urge to reach out to touch whatever had been released in the space between them.

He took his hat off, turning it slowly to a distant rhythm. 'Maybe it's about becoming what we consume, a song for a woman in translation.'

Back in London, Kara emerged from Forest Hill Overground station dishevelled, starving. Plane food had been paltry, inadequate. She remembered the strips of liquorice in her rucksack, followed by Kizzy's potent smile, the confession that he was of no fixed abode, that he liked to fly God's class rather than first, that he'd quipped of drinking juice from Banksia plants, instead of alcohol, that tasted like kangaroo piss.

Her stomach rumbled, punctuating the pattern of her thoughts. It was Saturday, the start of Open House week when people in Forest Hill received strangers into their homes to share artwork, conversation, music. Anything. The streets hummed with activity. In the station forecourt, she passed tables of free edible plants. Hordes of people gathered around them were resistant to an orderly queue, grabbing plants like okra, Winter Luxury pumpkin, dill, rosemary. Some children left their parents' sides, rushing to the ticket machines, pressing their hands against the screens as if gathering evidence of the day's journeys so far. They ran to the bikes under the shelter, leaning against each other in a false sense of stability. They circled the brightly painted piano, thrashing the keys in barely contained musical chaos before threading their way through the rest of the forecourt.

Kara reached inside her rucksack with tired hands, grabbing two strips of liquorice. She bent one playfully then bit into it, momentarily closing her eyes in delight as the sweet bitter taste flooded her tongue. On the Dartmouth Road where her flat was situated, she passed a mural of a giant white-haired woman in the clouds, surrounded by a fleet of red birds. The strip of liquorice melted into her blood. She popped another into her mouth. They were so moreish, she finished the packet right there on the street. In her suitcase, the bar outfit spilled a small electric horizon from the black shirt collar into a zip, an insect dead from shock in the bright light.

At the flat, she fell asleep in the bedroom. When she woke up, her body felt supple, soft, bendy, unfamiliar. She spotted a dark stain on the blue bed sheet. She looked at it with suspicion, rubbed the spot. Her fingers were black, liquorice-coloured, stretchy. Her heart rate tripled. She leaped off the bed somewhat unsteadily, rushed to the mauve bathroom. Skincare products lined the edges of the tub, crowded the sink. In her haste, she accidentally knocked over a bottle of Palmers Cocoa Butter. Her tooth-brush went flying.

She switched on the light. The 60-watt bulb stuttered in anticipation as she rushed to the mirror, light flickering sporadically as though arguing with itself. Chest heaving, she stared at her reflection, her breath pale magician's smoke. Sure enough she was not herself. Or she was herself but something different. Something skewed and accidental, something tainted with the margin particles of an incense-smelling man who could mimic the curves of a sidewinder. Her bathroom had become a circus balancing on two hinges, rocking unsteadily in the ether. She took tentative steps closer to the mirror. Sure enough she had transformed into liquorice, a black, sweet liquorice woman, a liquorice sweet black woman, bendy, stretchy, adaptable in harsh conditions, resplendent and irrepressible. Reconfigured heart oozing liquid midnight, necessary external jaggedness flung out like day traps, moist-turning tongue set anti-clockwise to catch soft light, soft memory, soft landing.

She turned the taps on for the sound of the sea to fill the sink and tub. All that came through was bursting, rushing water. She placed her hand under the cold tap, the weight of water bending her fingers slightly. She used her right hand to adjust them back, then raised both hands to water her head with night dew. She turned the cold tap off. The blast of hot water meant the pipes started whistling. Slowly, then speedily, panicked by the possibilities of changes tumbling through their lengthy, corroded bodies.

She pressed her fingers into her head, feeling her way around for a crack. Steam misted the mirror. She didn't want to melt. Melting meant not existing. She turned the hot-water tap off, waiting for the whistling to stop. She started screaming.

The fading sounds of the chugging pipes mutated into an alarm ringing in her head. Anxiety spread from the very heart of her, a burning sensation in her new body. Sydney had been a disaster. She was broken by it. Almost. She stepped back from the mirror, trying to weigh the ache within, the losses she'd left on Sydney Harbour turning to twisted currencies glowing in the dark, the octopus-shaped critter that had tried to gain entry to her suitcase to find a corner to possess. She pressed her mouth against that corner to breathe, to steady herself; loss of confidence, loss of income, loss of heart, loss of lover. The ache inside her grew into a kite-shaped slipstream spotted with silver. She started to cry, heaving sobs threatening to become accomplices in the cramped bathroom. She needed to fill the ache, to do something. It was Open House week after all. She grabbed a black bin bag from the top of the cabinet.

Around 1 a.m. she wandered the streets, bin bag in tow. Squishy sounds of her new limbs kept her company. She walked to the sprawling Horniman Museum gardens, found nothing to catch except the reflection of her old self in the café's glass doors and windows. That Kara had gone to Australia chasing a story: a dreadlocked molasses-hued man who believed his lost mother appeared to him during volcano eruptions, who took tender photographs that captured her silhouette exiting those eruptions. Kara had wanted to write his story but the man gave her heart to a volcano for his mother to eat.

On the steep London Road, she entered the white houses through windows left open. She gathered from the inhabitants things most people would never take during Open House: the post office clerk's fear of failure, the sweet-shop assistant's paranoia he'd die before doing half the items on his bucket list, the glint from the blade the kebab-shop owner used to carve scenes for three stillborn babies trapped in a revolving winter, the deli owner's conversations to the gremlin he'd transplanted into his chest that kept trying to break ceilings with a long, slimy tentacle. She wandered through houses while people slept, humming the tune Kizzy sang at the airport, leaving a trail of deep, warm sweetness, stuffing her bag until it was fit to burst.

When she arrived back home, the bin liner split on her bed, on the crumpled tulip-patterned duvet. The things she'd caught had charred wings and were flapping towards possible exits frenetically. White airbags sprang from the corners of her bed, shrieking incessantly before the air left them twisted into mean, sunken expressions. And the sharp pain exploding in Kara's chest before liquefying was unbearable.

The next morning, after discovering that a last self-collision resulted in change you couldn't foresee, Kara limped out onto the Dartmouth Road, having caught her left foot in a trap she'd flung from herself. She clutched her plane ticket to Sydney, a sacrificial woman in the heat hollering Kizzy's song about becoming what you eat. It was bright out. The day was alcoholic. As she sang, her body began to separate. Her head went first, tossed into the blind spot of a sputtering drunk holding a Guinness can like a lover. Her head shrank rapidly. Her legs came off, tumbling backwards into an argument between the off-licence owner and a woman holding a leash without a dog she claimed she'd lost at Heathrow airport.

Kara's golden eyes uprooted into the traffic, speedily rolling between lanes, between tyres, frantically blinking away images of a life that were discarded receipts for gutted angels with streaks of black tears on their faces, reduced to husks on the bent skyline. Her arms were dark boomerangs confused by an unplanned separation, the dizziness of slow traffic in the sky, attempting to embrace satellite dishes, antennas, and items that found their way to rooftops while the road swelled with resignation of a split. And a break somewhere that saw small creatures from accidents with Kara's last heartbeats mutating in their chests as they scurried onto the pavements on either side, leaving patches of unleaded fuel and kaleidoscopic red in their attempts to talk.

People from cafés and the boutique village-like stores and eateries, including the Hill Lounge and Kitchen and Bird in Hand, spilled out onto the street, watching. Two assistants from Sugar Mountain sweet shop abandoned its light, tantalising atmosphere of deep booths, board games and seductive retro sweets in large jars. They rushed out carrying a jar each to catch bits of Kara's body. Individuals from Forest Hill Pools filed out barefoot onto the pavement still in their costumes, dripping translucent daydreams doubling as swimming strokes beneath the sun. The locals were chess pieces held still by a human combustion on a glimmering day. Kara's thighs spun. One slid down a lamppost, leaving a dark, honey-like trail before becoming stuck at the bottom. The other slid across the window display of Il Mirto's Italian Deli and Ice Cream store. Her head now reduced to pulp was being lapped up in abandon by the drunk on all fours. His tongue darting greedily, the Guinness can forgotten, squashed under his knee, pennies spilling from his pocket, like a marauding coppery fountain.

Kara's mouth was sylph-like, chased by an Aboriginal cowboy's hat into the distance before it melted onto the rim in the shape of an atom bursting, an accidental decoration. Her scattered teeth were white jewels for the afternoon. A man in a diving costume caught her vagina, sucking on it, the nectar of a goddess. Her hands were clasped together, prayer-like, while bits of clouds morphed into the shapes of temporary pale clothing for the inhabitants of Forest Hill to wear as the uniform of witnesses. After their naïve prayer, her hands eventually melted on the wheel of a dented blue Ford Cortina that, later, would run out of fuel. And all that was left was the morning to come. All that was left was her torso on the edge: black, gleaming, edible, sweet. Liquorice sweet. Full of warped, rhapsodic song in the traffic.

Filamo

The last monk told the tongue that holding a naked sheep's head underwater would undo it all. Some time before that, prior to the madness beginning, old Barking Abbey loomed in the chasm; grey, weather worn, remote. Inside the Abbey, a tongue sat in the golden snuffbox on an empty long dining table; pink, scarred and curled into a ruffled silken square of night. The previous week, the tongue had been used as a bookmark in a marked, leather-bound King James Bible, page 45, where the silhouette of a girl had been cut out, loaded with words like *high*, *hog*, *clitoris*, *iodine*, *cake*, its moist tip glistening in temporary confinement. The week before that, the tongue had been left in the fountain at the back of the Abbey between winking coins. There, it pressed its tip to a stray ripple, cold and malleable, shaping it into a weight, pulling it down, under, up again. Several weeks back, it had been in a hallway window, leaning into Mary's hands whose fingertips tasted of a charred foreign footprint from the grass. Her fingertips had sensed a change in the air before the monks came, when the corridors were quiet, expectant. And molecules had shifted in preparation for a delivery. The monks arrived through a hole in time on a cold, misty morning, transported via a warp in space that mangled the frequencies of past and present. They had arrived curling hands that did not belong to them. Unaware that this would have consequences none foresaw except a tongue bending in the background, unaware of the repercussions of time travelling.

Each time the tongue was moved, it lost a sentence. The monks missed this in their ritual of silence. They had done for weeks, walking around rooms with arms behind their backs, bodies shrouded in heavy brown robes, shaven sunken heads soft to the touch. They trod this new ground carrying yolks in their mouths, hardening as morning became noon, noon became evening, and evening became night.

One morning, the monks found a miller's wife gutted on the stone wall enclosing the allotment, a white felt cap shoved into her mouth, her husband's initials embroidered in blue at the top right corner of her bloody apron: V.O. They threw salt on her skin. The tongue tasted the sharpness, and that night, Dom Vitelli made the noise of a kettle boiling in his sleep. He began to tremble, covered with a cold sweat. He fell to the floor, stuck.

The next morning, the monks rose to discover the empty

well near the stone outbuilding surrounded by plump, purple jabuticaba fruit, tender and bruised, the colour dwindling in areas as though a god was sucking it through a crack in the sky. Lonely figures in their heavy brown robes, the monks held their hands out as they circled the Abbey. They heard the sounds of buses on the high street, car doors slammed shut, trains grinding to a halt. They caught items that fell through noise, things they had never seen: a white adapter plug from the sound of a plane speeding through the sky, a black dog muzzle Dom Oman later took to wearing sitting by the fountain, a knuckle duster that fell from the sound of a baby crying. They placed these items at the altar in the chapel, flanked on either side by candles whose blue flames bent, then shrank sporadically. They took turns holding their palms over the flames. By the time the monks began their chores, the cockerel that had fallen over the walls from a car horn began to smash its beak into a jabuticaba fruit. Afterwards, it jumped into the stream connected to the Roding river, following a thinning yellow light it attempted to chase into the next day.

The tongue was warm in Filamo's pocket, pressed against a copper coin bearing the number two in roman lettering. The musty taste lingered of old items passing through. Filamo, a cloaked figure, a betrayer among the monks, stood outside the prayer room, fingering a swelling on the tongue, listening quietly. Dom Emmanuel paced inside, the only other place speaking was permitted, aside from supper, during this imposed period of silence. A slightly forlorn figure, he shook. The bald patch on his head looked soft, like a newborn's. Light streamed through the stained-glass window where three naked cherubs wore angry, adult expressions and had changed positions again overnight. One lay on its side holding an ear, the other was eating stigmata injuries and the third at the bottom left corner had tears running down its cheeks into the jabuticaba fruit growing through its chest. Dom Emmanuel faced the silence of the cross on the nave wall without the figure of Christ, which had turned up at supper two days before, bleeding between slices of bread. There were three deep wooden pews behind the Dom, as if half-heartedly built, the seating scratched. Dom Emmanuel began to walk back and forth. Then he paused momentarily as though to catch his breath, chest rising and falling. He held out his arms, confessing that lately he had begun to worry about his lover withering in a wormhole. The man Dom Emmanuel loved had not made it through this time, stuck in a winter that would quickly ice his organs and distribute the seven languages he spoke into the orbit for other monks to grab and stow away along with new disguises.

Dom Emmanuel could feel that cold in his bones, an absence of language, lightness in his tongue. Recently, Dom Emmanuel had dreamed of them running through lush, sunlit fields naked, penises limp at first, then turgid, moist at the tips till thick spurts of sperm dribbled and their irises glinted. He missed the warmth of holding another body skin to skin, the innocence of early youth, the freedom of making mistakes. He moaned that his hands ached, that they had begun to talk to him, consumed by restlessness, till he sat up in bed sweating, tense, listening to a distant mangled cry travelling towards his organs, to his hands. For days the cry had come to him each night while the others slept, on each occasion magnified by the constant silence, taut, suffocating. The cry grew in volume, weight, intent, till he was led by it, until he found himself stumbling outside into the grounds, disrobing by the darkened stream gleaming in the night. Naked, covered with bite marks, he hunched down to catch things from the water: Siamese green lizards who shared an Adam's apple, a piece of jabuticaba fruit, which grew another layer of purple skin each time you touched it, one cherub whose eyes had blackened from things it had witnessed upstream, a lung wrapped in clingfilm. Surrounded by his discontented small audience, Dom Emmanuel removed the clingfilm, crying as he ate flesh. It tasted like a man he once paid four gold coins in Tenochtitlan to keep him company, to be rough then tender with him afterwards, who had stuck his curious tongue into his armpits as if digging for his body's secrets using a pliable instrument. Dom Emmanuel did not turn around when Filamo moved towards him lifting the blade. The cut to his neck was swift. He fell to the floor, blood gushing. The cry from his lips was familiar. It had been chasing him for days. He pressed his hands desperately against his neck, attempting to catch one last item rising through the blood. Dom Emmanuel died thinking of his lover's sour mouth, praying into it. The wound on his neck a cruel smile, clutching the lines of an old rectory sign bearing roman number two in the left corner, his talking, gnarled hands slowly eroding. And half his body purple from a winter he already knew. While the monks scattered in shock, the tongue inherited Dom Emmanuel's last words *El Alamein*.

When the saints arrived through their time cannon, continuing their ancient tradition as watchmen over the monks, the night was onyx-shaped. A faint howl followed them onto the tower. The Abbey was formidable in the moonlight; imposing, damp, grey, surrounded by high stone walls. The saints were orange-skinned from the festival of memory. Each had a feature missing but something to replace it within their bodies. St Peter was missing an ear, yet had a small translucent dragon's wing growing against a rib. St Augustine had lost a finger on his left hand but had two hearts, one pumping blood, the other mercury, so much so his tongue became silvery at particular angles. St Christopher had lost an eye and gained a filmy yellow fish iris, which cried seawater no matter his mood. This time, each had been fired from a cannon. Temporarily deaf, they clutched instructions for short transformations in golden envelopes. They wandered the cold halls lined with carvings and paintings on the walls, while the monks were gathered at supper, oblivious.

The saints deposited the envelopes beneath their beds. Each individual instruction for transformation sealed, yet written in the same long, right-leaning handwriting by the same white feather dipped in blue ink. Each slip of yellow paper wrinkled at the corners, worn from weather, prayer, silence. Then the saints fashioned three flagpoles from sticks they found in the cellar. They planted them on the grounds. The blue flag for go, red for pause, breathe, green for transform. Afterwards, on their journey back to two golden towers erected between wormholes, the saints became infants in the wind.

Later that night, the remaining Doms filed from the front of the Abbey holding their golden envelopes. Dom Ruiz led the way, stopping to take his position at the green flagpole. The other Doms followed. Dom Mendel, slighter than the rest, took a breath on the steps by the Roding river's stream. The white hexagon several feet from the flagpoles spun seductively. In the library window, old leather-bound books nursed the wisdom of hands slowly erased by time. The Doms took their positions on all fours. Light trickles of dark rain began to fall. They uttered, '*Pater tollis peccata.*'

Their mouths distorted. The bell rang. They darted forward, towards the centre and each other, growling. A sharp, splintered pain shot through their heads. Spots of white appeared in their vision. Bones cracked as they expanded, organs grew, teeth lengthened, fur sprouted, hoofs appeared, nostrils widened. Their sense of smell heightened. Dom Ruiz became a boar lunging at Dom Mendel, the centaur, chasing him with an urgency that had his teeth chattering. Dom Kamil became an epicyon hunting Dom Augustine, the procoptodon, between all three flagpoles, through the other side of the white hexagon where the static hissed, then back up again. They snarled at the skyline, leaping, rushing, following the strong scent of old flesh emanating from the soil. They buried their faces in it, dug, leaving large prints around the Abbey that had a peculiar beauty from above. Three hours later, they retreated to their starting positions, becoming men again, exhausted bodies heaving. Speckles of blood fell on the golden envelopes, over the lines in foreign hands that had arranged into blueprints.

There were always injuries during a transformation. But the small, morphing nuclei they had generated would flatten in their brains, rising again when necessary, mimicking the silhouettes of tiny watchmen. As their breathing steadied, they studied the red flag flapping in the wind for stop.

After the transformation, the silence within the Abbey was heavier, loaded. Having been banished by the saints for the fallen monk in their midst, each monk was busy dealing with the repercussions of their borrowed hands. And who knew what that could do to a man? Seeds of doubt and mistrust had begun to take root in this fertile ground of the unspoken, watered by the saliva of sealed envelopes. The monks did not venture beyond the Abbey, afraid of being sucked into a vacuum of noise they would not recognise. Noises of a future they felt unprepared for, frightened that the influences of an outside world would somehow shorten their time at the Abbey. Everything they needed was within the Abbey's walls. They grew their own food using the allotment at the back. At least twelve chickens were enough to feed from for a while, producing eggs for breakfast and the occasional comic attempt at escape. One chicken laid ten eggs that would not hatch, each filled with a finger of a new monk poking through deep red yolks. And somehow the Jesus figurine had found its way to these eggs. Stained with mud, it sat among them as they rolled and the other chickens leaped over the sound. Fed on bits of sullied bread, little Jesus waited patiently for a different kind of resurrection.

The saints made several visits back to the Abbey through their time cannon to deliver items: salt, a bow and arrow, a television remote, nails, a hammer, three serrated knives. Several days after the transformation, Dom Augustine woke in the middle of the night barking, like a dog, tongue slightly distended, skin clammy. The next morning, he began to set animal traps around the grounds; one on top of the tower, one in the allotment, one behind the middle pew in the prayer room, under his bed, one on the white hexagon slowly fading from damp and cold. After all, who knew what a man's shadow would do while he pretended to look the other way? Dom Augustine felt panic rising inside him. Each day his tongue loosened further, as if it would fall out at any moment. He did not know whether it was his increasingly intensified barking at nights that was the cause or his particular kink from banishment, from flight. There were always complications. He had arrived in the main chapel, between two tall marble grey pillars, deposited on the alabaster altar, naked and wrapped in a thin silvery film reflecting past angles of light. His limbs had hurt, his head throbbed. His breaths were slow, deep, attempting to acclimatise. He had broken through the film, instinctively grabbing at items from a past that would never appear, knocking over two large white candlesticks on either side. Famished, he scrambled along the cold altar. He looked down; his gaze met the knowing blue eyes of a cherub, who jumped up and down excitedly, showing him its scarred back from repeatedly falling through stained-glass windows. Its mouth was purple after eating a combination of plump fruits and unidentifiable things. He'd had to break his hands in just like all the other Doms: carving a small Jesus figurine, fixing the hole in the cellar roof, building a pantry. The ache in his hands never fully left, only dulling with time. His fear of items and sounds from the outside threatening to infiltrate the Abbey had become so potent: one afternoon he had been washing his hands in holy water by the pantry when the sound of an axe lifting, falling, chopping, breaking, smashing had almost deafened him. Slow at first, coming from afar. Then closer, louder, heavier till he curled up by the metallic bowl of water screaming then barking, breaking the silence.

A week after Dom Augustine set the animal traps, parts of his body were found in each trap. Pieces in the traps by the fading white hexagon looked like an offering. The axe the saints delivered had vanished. The tongue in Filamo's pocket dined on splattered blood.

It was a chilly evening on the occasion Dom Kamil decided to perform his act of rebellion against the silence. A light frost covered the grounds, more jabuticaba fruits from the well scattered. Large pillars at the Abbey's entrance bore tiny cracks oozing a sticky, thin sap. The intricate golden chapel ceiling, depicting Old Testament scenes, began to shed tiny specks of gold from the corners. Only an observant eye would notice the figures had begun to head in the opposite direction. Metallic bowls of holy water carefully placed outside room entrances collected reflections as if they were a currency. Dom Kamil awoke to find himself doused in kerosene and Doms Ruiz and Mendel absent. Throat dry, he trembled before swinging his feet over the bed onto the floor. The smell of kerosene was acrid. He did not call out. Instead, he slipped on his dull, weighty brown cloak, briefly running a hand over the length of wooden flute he'd kept close during the daytimes. For weeks he had found the silence unbearable, craving the joy music brought. He had resorted to wandering around the Abbey with the flute he'd made secretly, rubbing his hands along it when his fingers curled and flexed with intent. Beyond the Abbey walls, an ambulance siren wailed. Dom Kamil rushed outside. At least fifty yellow notes were strewn on the frosted ground. He scrambled between each one, eagerly opening them but they were mockingly empty. Distraught, he pulled the flute from his pocket and began to play. When Filamo set him alight he did not stop, playing urgently until he fell to his knees, the heat of the flames licking his skin, veins, blinding him. The sound of the flute hitting cold ground reverberated in the abyss, the ambulance siren shattered. A dark curl of smoke shrank into the tongue poking out contemptuously from Filamo's pocket.

The next morning, the two remaining Doms wandered the halls with the taste of kerosene in their mouths.

On the fated Sunday that followed, Dom Ruiz and Dom Mendel began their last set of chores for the week orchestrated by the saints, setting scenes for destruction: ripping

the pages of books in the library, defacing the expressions
of religious figures in paintings hanging on walls, smashing up the organ nobody had been allowed to play in the
chapel, flinging the black and white keys over the bodies
of ten monks in the deep, open grave tucked behind the
stone steps. They sprinkled salt on those bodies. And when
those monks' mouths were sealed shut again by snow from
a future winter, they fed the chickens communion. After
dyeing the underside of their tongues purple, they fished
out the animal traps, assembling them into a circle at the
Abbey's entrance because their hands could not help themselves. They danced within the circle until sweat ran down
their backs, till their legs ached and the skyline became a
blur. The nuclei embedded in their brains rose, bubbled,
spat. They danced for what felt like eternity until finally
they crawled indoors. Heavy-eyed and wary of collapsing
in their sleeping quarters, they sat across from each other
at the long dining table, watching, waiting. They dared
not sleep, until the saint in their peripheral vision began
to scream, burning bright, burnished orange smog into
their heads.

Dawn arrived to discover Dom Ruiz slung over the bell,
hands clinging limply to a thick white rope, face battered
beyond recognition. He dangled like a grisly gift a god had
dispatched. Meanwhile the tongue ran its moist tip along
the bruises on Filamo's hands.

*

Spat out from another chasm, Dom Mendel lay sprawled on a wide patch of the Abbey's green surrounded by concrete paths. Time travel flight had occurred again. He knew it from the trembling in his knees, the ache spreading in his chest, the blockage in his ears slowly thinning, popping. His bruised hands were numb, stiff after being curled in the same position for hours. As though he'd been inserted into a corner of sky trying to balance, fingers instinctively wrapping around the shadows of lost items. Every junction fell off the map each time, a severed organ floating in white smoke till it disappeared. He sat up gingerly, taking small gulps of air. It felt like spring. Bright sunlight shrouded everything. The Abbey was a carcass of its former self, its high walls reduced to mere remains. The sound of cars on the roads around it was jarring, alien. Mouth dry, barefoot, he stood slowly, noting the curfew tower in the distance. Exits at either end of the gutted green gladiator-like pit beckoned. He decided to take the exit in front rather than the one behind him. He crossed some stone steps before landing in the graveyard. St Margaret's Church stood to his right behind the tower a short walk away, bearing a flimsy white banner that said *Café Open*. People passed him, throwing curious looks. Their clothing appeared odd and unfamiliar. He ran his hands over a few gravestones. The rough stone was cold to the touch. He grabbed sprigs of grass lining the bases, placed them on his tongue. Chewing, he made his way over the zebra crossing and onto the tail end of the market on East Street, drawn by the buzz of stalls, the cacophony of voices, the smell of meat hissing and spitting over a barbecue. He ran a finger over the tongue in his pocket as he heard the words *bell end, mango, fireworks, truncheon.* It curled against his finger as though acknowledging receipt. He walked along the market in shock, throngs of bodies spilling, multiplying and scurrying in every direction. On the high street, a man held a snarling Alsatian back from him. He could smell what it had eaten hours ago, a rotten, pungent scent. He resisted the urge to bare his teeth. Something lodged in his chest. His blood warmed. His heart began to mutate into the shape of the snarling dog's mouth, knocking against chest walls. He stumbled away from them. Trapped light in his eye split into tiny grains. Everything felt intense, gauzy. A bearded man bumped into him. He entered the sliding red door of the shopping centre almost by accident. Things bled into each other: the mannequins' mouths pressed against their glass confines, stitches from their hands coming undone, grazing his retinas. Along the way his footsteps were dogged by sightings of familiar faces. Dom Emmanuel appeared on the raised stage for a concert, holding the knife that had killed him, slicing his neck repeatedly at the microphone. Dom Augustine's head lay in the Asda supermarket freezer, one animal trap snapping over his lost limbs as they reappeared. Dom Kamil sat engulfed in flames in a barber's chair. Dom Ruiz lay slumped over a *Thomas the Tank Engine* train, clutching one yellow note.

Dom Mendel passed a line of monks on an escalator, touching their shoulders, but each one vanished. He was consumed by a feeling of loneliness so vast it was unknowable in this lifetime. He followed the exit out and back onto the streets. He kept walking, filled with a slow hypnotic wonder, wiping the dew off a car side mirror, becoming a small figure in its contained distances. Then on all fours, he scavenged in the bins outside the Yaki Noodle bar opposite the station. Afterwards, he walked around back streets staring at houses. He walked to Creekmouth, passing the mural of two men vomiting water coddling ships while the land flooded. He studied the parked HGVs on industrial roads, wondering what they contained, noticing the small factories and recycling stations. A veil of bleakness cloaked it all. The ghosts of Creekmouth swirled. Workers for the Lawes Chemical and Fertiliser Company emerged from rows of cottages attempting to stuff items into his pockets. The Bluebird and the Yellow Peril aircraft of the Handley Page factory hovered above, between the rough marshland of Barking creek and the north bank of the Thames, leaving white trails in the sky. Children ran from the school, mouths turning to dust as their cries faded. Debris of old lives tumbled through the nearby tidal barrier. The sound of ships sinking filled his ears. An ache in his hands intensified. Laughter from Romanian weddings rang at the entrance to the River Restaurant. He almost walked in to search for hands he could borrow. He stood in the midst of it all, listening to past surrounding marshy land rising, urged by the echoes of the Thames, to the sound of a great flood coming. He did not notice his feet were bleeding. His teeth began to chatter, his tongue distended. The tongue in his pocket started talking.

The last Dom, Dom Mendel stood on the bank of the Roding river, disrobing to reveal breasts jutting, her nipples hardening in the cold. Pregnant with another bloody season, her new name carved on her stomach from a serrated knife read: Filamo. She had left behind the Abbey in the chasm, its entrances spitting Bible sheets, its lines leaning against a distant prayer, the faces of saints morphing into bruises. A different transformation was occurring: malevolent cherubs chased the cockerel; the limping cockerel, drunk from holy water, chased the Jesus figurine, squawking, 'Amen!' Rolling jabuticaba fruit chased the hatched monk's fingers. And the Abbey chased new burial ground. Dom Filamo listened to the symphony of cars, human traffic, the beauty of noise. She dipped her left foot into the water. After fishing a hammer and tongue from her robe pockets, she started to bludgeon her head, hitting the ring of hair. As another yolk broke and blood ran down her face, she slipped the tongue into her mouth howling. The tongue of a saint. That first kill. The reason for the punishment of a period of silence. Her skin mottled. She leaped into the river gripping the hammer, chasing the sheep's head that had surely become a different animal by now.

Point and Trill

From the steep road nestled between the valleys near Llanberis, the warmly lit cabins of the distance appeared to be floating in darkness. Lights flickered as though they were blinking. Gill allowed himself the luxury of imagining what lay in wait. He shifted the gearstick into fourth, hit the accelerator, breathing out slowly. He turned to Bronwyn, who was staring out of the window at cloaks of darkness shifting off undulating green mounds into restless costumes. Lately, her mood swings had fluctuated from one extreme to the other. He couldn't quite pinpoint what he'd done, when her dissatisfaction had crept in, a loose wire sparking between their movements. They'd become one of those couples they thought they'd never be: increasingly distant. In the beginning, they'd jokingly referred to their union as what pi is to pi: two irrational numbers finding a shared circumference. He took in her profile: the patrician nose, deep shadows under emerald eyes that had bewitched him at first, the shock of long, dark hair swishing carelessly down one shoulder. Their Vauxhall Cavalier shuddered over a dip as they passed the sign reading *Coetrioedd I fyny Ymlaen* (woodlands up ahead).

Married for five years, they'd met during a Guggenheim fellowship, she for marine biology, and he for his work as an eel ecologist. Uncannily, they each had one American parent. He'd been writing a research paper on the rapidly declining *Anguilla anguilla*, which had once flourished in London's rivers. At the time, he was quietly impressed by her. Intelligent but not showy, she wielded a sarcastic tongue with an unapologetic Welsh accent and seemed endlessly curious about the world. Their passionate trysts had peppered his studies of eel migration at sites across the country. Now, some of those eels swam back to the car's side mirrors, contorting their bodies, threatening to break the glass with their knowledge.

'I watched a male seahorse giving birth before lunch the other day,' he offered enthusiastically. 'Incredible, literally shooting those babies out of its stomach. Made me wonder if men were able to give birth whether the world would be a better place.'

Bronwyn scoffed, adjusted herself in her seat. 'If men could give birth they'd be even worse. You'd have hormonal Trumps and Gadaffys. Imagine. This is ridiculous. Why are we going paintballing at night?' she asked, suddenly glaring at him.

He indicated left, turning smoothly, a mischievous glint in his gold-flecked brown eyes. 'Because it's fun and a little primal. Ziggy should be there already.'

'Speaking of infants,' she said, popping a mint into her mouth. She glanced at the rear-view mirror, as if expecting a passenger made of exhaust-pipe smoke in the back seat.

'I don't understand why you've always had an issue with him. I don't get to see him that often any more,' Gill said almost sulkily.

She opened the dashboard compartment, fished out an old issue of the *New Scientist*, flicked through its pages. 'He's a prick. He makes me uncomfortable. That's the problem with you. You never see people as they really are.'

They arrived at their location a short while later. Gill steered the car steadily towards the cluster of cabins. The sky yawned dots of light; the moon seemed forlorn and magisterial. Beyond them, the woodlands hummed seductively, cloaked in a dense darkness. Bronwyn undid her seatbelt, listening to it snap back. She returned the copy of the *New Scientist* to the glove compartment, slipped on her worn brown Converses. Something landed on the car's bonnet with a thwack, teeth flashing white at them through the windscreen glass. They jerked back. Gill stopped the car, switched the engine off.

'What the hell was that?' he asked. Subdued light from the small icons by the steering wheel waned.

'This is why we shouldn't have come. I'm not getting hurt on this trip just because you and Ziggy want to be juvenile man babies for the night,' Bronwyn hissed, the angry curl of her mouth somehow more charged than whatever was waiting in the dark.

They hadn't even been fucking lately but the possibility of imminent danger stirred Gill's blood. He kissed her swiftly, his boyishly handsome face breaking into a smile. 'Does that comment even make sense? Don't get your Welsh panties into a twist, my sweet.' He grabbed a crowbar from under his seat, hopped out of the car, slowly approaching the bonnet. Whatever it was hadn't moved. He gripped the crowbar tightly. It felt rough against his skin where it had rusted. The wind howled, giving voice to the anxieties dormant in his brain: Bronwyn's edginess, her worry over the last paper she'd had to write on fossil marine life. Three weeks ago, he'd woken in the early hours of the morning to find her at the opposite corner of the bed, legs splayed, scratching the inside of her elbow in a trance, like a toy perched and wound up on his bed to repeat the same action. He had to hold her under the cold shower for several minutes before she snapped out of it, spluttering, swearing, kicking at him, as the slow sounds of their London street awakening filtered through the bathroom window. Red mist from her eyes had seeped into his skin.

Since then, there'd been two more trance episodes. One at Morrison's where she'd walked into the back-room freezer sniffing cold cuts of meat, several packets under her arm, the other at the Hunterian Museum. He'd left her to use the toilet, returning to find she'd removed a baby bat from a jar on display. She cradled it gently, staring at it, as if it were a thing of wonder. The liquid it was preserved in spilled onto her green skirt, spreading into a large patch, which dogged them for the rest of the day. Worried her trances were some sort of response to stress and anxiety, he'd called a neurologist friend, who hadn't been able to give him any definitive answers. *Make sure she gets enough sleep, exercise, eats properly. If it gets worse, go to the GP first,* that sort of generic, non-specific advice.

The bonnet wasn't dented from what he could see. His shoulders shook with mirth. Its sharp-toothed mouth was still. Dead still. There was rustling as Ziggy emerged from the side chuckling, his lean, wiry frame in full view. He aimed his flashlight at Gill, then Bronwyn, who shook her head.

'The master of ceremonies welcomes you. You killed the wolf rug,' Ziggy said, smiling affectionately at Gill. He walked towards Bronwyn, rapped on the window. Tugging the Mussolini mask on his head further back, he breathed against the glass. A ring of mist formed, a third murky mouth between them waiting to grab at stray threads before disappearing. A black whistle dangled against his chest. His green checked shirt was rolled up at the sleeves. Of the two men, Ziggy was the more rugged. His grey eyes tended to look cold even when he laughed. His unruly dark curls were scraped back. He possessed weathered, large hands and a knowing gaze. As if you were an artichoke whose layers his fingers had peeled off, whose heart he'd already eaten. Bronwyn smiled tensely. The half-bitten artichoke heart inside her floated up to the sound of a shrill, garbled whistle. She stuck a middle finger up at him, grabbed the bright patchwork-style small rucksack at her feet, stepped out of the car.

'You should see your face when you're frightened,' Ziggy said, by way of greeting, reaching for the rucksack, which she deftly strapped onto her back. Gill popped the boot open, stowed the crowbar before grabbing the offending wolf rug. It had one fang missing. She took the rug off Gill. 'What was that story you shared with me about you and Ziggy trapped in some caves when you were kids and Ziggy shitting himself?'

'Hey! That was told to you in confidence,' Gill said, slightly embarrassed, face flushed.

Ziggy patted Gill on the back in brotherly solidarity. 'You should know Gill can be prone to exaggerating. Our coupling was so much more blissful before she arrived,' he joked, shooting Bronwyn a hardened stare that implied he was anything but amused. Gill threw her an impatient look.

Oh, shit. She'd forgotten. The day the boys had been trapped in the caves, Ziggy had discovered his mother was dying from liver cancer that morning.

She glanced up. The moon was gauzy. She wondered if the guys had noticed.

She looked into the deadened eyes of the wolf rug, picturing its chest pregnant with creatures that would end up contained in glass jars, breathing in off-white liquids before taking flight in her hands, breaking through a watery ceiling. She hated unevenness: it was unfair. She plucked the fang from the left side of its mouth, stroking it before slipping it into her pocket.

Ziggy had just been fucking before he met them. She could smell it on him.

She inhaled.

She left them talking and smoking outside. Inside their cabin, she dumped her rucksack and the rug on the bed. She checked for exits, a ritual she performed whenever she stayed somewhere new. There were two: the front entrance and a back door through a tiny kitchen area. The cabin was cosy, threadbare. She suspected the other five cabins would be similar. She opened the dresser by the bed, found a bottle of Black Bush Irish whiskey. She unscrewed the cap, took a long swig, feeling the aftershock of heat burning her throat. The roaring fire spat. She sat on the bed, bouncing slowly, testing its spring. Removing her shirt, she felt her skin warming even more. Her tongue, a little distended, stung. She took another gulp of whiskey before setting it on top of the dresser beside a hand-drawn map of the area. Ziggy's touch, no doubt. She took off her Converses, enjoying the immediate relief, lifted the mattress, found an open packet of Durex Light condoms. She ran her finger over the diameter, looked inside: three left from a stash of five. She pictured the two missing condoms stretching in the doorway, filling with tiny lost items. She fished a small makeup mirror from her rucksack, held it up to her tongue. The right underside had darkened, as though bruised. Her tongue was longer. She dropped the mirror on the bed. Fed the fire a couple more logs. Lying on the floor, she pressed her ear to it, listening to the sounds of the undergrowth coming through the floorboards. Then she unclipped her bra. Topless, she watched the guys from the window. They were talking animatedly, Gill's hands gesticulating wildly, Ziggy listening with an intense expression on his face. Gill removed a folded photo from his pocket. Their dark heads crouched over it, laughing. Partially obscured by the white curtain, Bronwyn turned from the window. A log crackled, popped. The flames curled.

The way Gill told the story, the boys had gone into the secret caves at Lydstep Cliffs on a dare. Ziggy had bet him two *Beano* comics and his mountain bike on loan for a day he wouldn't see it through. And Gill, never one to back down from a challenge, had agreed. The boys were similar in athletic ability but Ziggy had the edge as a better swimmer while Gill was agile, light on his feet. They'd gone in egging each other on. It was late afternoon; the caves seemed cavernous, dark and deceptive. Like the further you went in the more dimensions you'd find. Forty feet below, a crystal blue lake beckoned, a watery eye leaking slowly into the cracks. They'd left their bikes at the cave's opening, which looked like two hands in prayer; their wheels spun against its ceremonies of feet sinking into sand. Ziggy had been in a strange mood all day, reckless, more so than usual. The cold hit them first, as if the caves hadn't let a past winter out of their clutches. There was evidence of vagrants passing through: a soiled sleeping bag in a corner, a few heroin needles, an old wind jacket, empty beer cans. Damp fossils between the rocks gleamed as the boys climbed down slowly, Gill ahead. Ziggy cracked a joke about their supplementary science teacher, Mrs Gaskill. Distracted, Gill slipped, hurtling down. Sheer terror gripped him. His throat constricted so tightly he couldn't scream. It happened in split seconds. His bomber jacket billowing, the flutter of a *Beano* comic falling out, coins spilling from his pocket, Ziggy leaping off the rocks in pursuit, the breaking of water, the discovery that falling into water from a great height was painful. Gill hit the water hard, went down. He tried to swim up but couldn't, arms flailing. His trainer laces were caught on a rock. He attempted to free himself. He couldn't reach properly. His chest was filling with water. Pain shot through his left leg. He couldn't hold his breath much longer. Through the panic underwater, he saw Ziggy swimming towards him. He untangled him, removing the offending black Nike trainer, which began to tumble down towards the murky bottom. They each broke the surface gasping, heaved their bodies onto the edge, coughing. Gill's teeth chattered; his body shook so much he thought the chill would never leave him. Ziggy turned to him, holding his contentious black footwear like a flag. 'I told you the drop was crazy. The old crow's dying, cancer,' he said, throwing the trainer at Gill. Above them, one heroin needle pierced the trapped winter. The other cried blue water.

There were three other couples: Ludwig and Eno, Gael and Marcella, and Brandon and Noel, who'd driven down from Edinburgh. None of the couples knew each other. They gathered in the area before the cabins, dressed in camouflage clothing. Ziggy handed them the guns, explained the rules of the game. The aim was to take out every other couple. Not just one member, both of them. They were allowed to venture as deeply as they liked into the surrounding woods. Whichever couple won had to signal this by firing three shots into the air. They tested their guns on a few trees, the pop of shots ringing loudly. Explosions of colour decorated those trees as if they'd produced bright gateways to walk through. Bronwyn signalled to Gill she needed to use the loo. She left the others, walked back to their cabin. The weight of the gun in her hands was an anchor, the cold night air on her neck crisp, the tiredness from hours of travelling slowly leaving her limbs. At their cabin she used the toilet, the rush of water flushing the only accompanying sound to her movements. In the mirror, she held the torchlight against her mouth, lifting her tongue. The bruise had expanded, a small ragged shadow stuck to the underside of her tongue. She flicked the torch off. In the bedroom, she noticed a small white tub buried far back under the bed. She hadn't spotted it before. She pulled it out, lifted the lid. A dark, bubbling concoction filled the container. She took a sniff. It smelt like eels, puréed eels. She started to feel feverish, heady. She took another deep sniff. The pungent smell went straight to her brain. The frothy liquid abyss continued to bubble. Intrigued, she stuck her fingers in.

She pressed her tongue against them. It tasted salty, fishy and alcoholic. It tasted like the dark corner of a lost memory. She licked her fingers clean. Her hands trembled. In haste, she knocked the container, spilling some of its contents over the gun. She buried her face in the tub, licking frantically. Midway through, she spotted it, like a smile folded into a crevice: the missing wolf tooth rising through the froth, pointed, jagged and definite. She held it tenderly, careful not to drop it, a diamond pressed against her heartbeat. The bruised shadow left her tongue to throw handfuls of colour at the leaky moon.

*

Four hours had passed, still no sign of Bronwyn. As Gill wound his way further into the woods, he felt a knot of worry growing in his gut. He couldn't call because in keeping with the rules of the game all mobile phones had been left at the main cabins. What if she'd gone into another trance and didn't know what the fuck was happening? What if she was injured, somehow unable to signal for help? What if she'd decided to head back to London after all, fed up with the weekend already? He weighed each possibility with concern. The problem with Bronwyn was, lately he never knew how she'd react in any given situation. While this had been attractive initially, he now found it tiresome. The longer they were together, the less he felt he knew her. He tugged the gun strap further up his shoulder; some twigs snapped beneath his feet. In the distance, a loud pop sounded in the air. He looked up, watching the darkness of the sky as if a firework had splintered into the shape of a clue. Scurrying through the trees alerted him, then waned into nothing. The temperature had dropped considerably. His breath blew out in puffs of mist to which the surroundings adjusted. He needed to keep moving to stay warm. Earlier, he'd shot Eno in the back; Eno had played dead, neon paint splattered onto the back of his jacket, amusingly curling into a foetal position before springing up again, then diving for cover as Gill fired more shots. Gill had allowed him to run off. That had been hours ago. He hadn't spotted Ludwig or the others yet. He rummaged inside his trouser pocket, shoved a stick of gum into his mouth, pulled out a photo. He smiled, nursing the warmth of the memory. It was an old picture of him and Ziggy with the rugby team at the pub. They were eighteen, still in their uniforms. They'd just beaten the team from St Albans. The boys were laughing, holding up a trophy and a ball. The slight figure of their mascot in a gecko costume stood beside them wearing a white T-shirt that read *No Exit*. Gill could never remember who their mascot had been. Weathered lines sprang from a few heads, drunken celluloid lightning. Then the lines became lanes, the boys in one, the trophy and rugby ball in another, the mascot in the third rushing towards each other, while a new kind of weather swirled beneath the subdued pub lighting. Gill ran his hands over those lines, closed his eyes. He flicked them open. In the photo, they were now all neon foetuses curled into submission; the trophy and the ball spun in the middle. The mascot costume sagged from a body that had left it.

He came upon a stone cabin unexpectedly. The surrounding trees seemed to lean towards each other conspiratorially. Gill fished out a miniature bottle of vodka from the inside pocket of his jacket, knocked some back, enjoying the snaky liquid warming his throat. This cabin was much older than the rustic offerings the group were staying at. It veered slightly to the left, as if it had tried to escape the spot but remained in the end. An old, broken antenna was on the roof, dilapidated from storing the movements of passers-by. One brown hiking boot with undone laces lay next to it. Wild brushes crawled up the cabin, shrivelled tips bending as though dipping into a chasm the eye couldn't see. *The point* was written on a large piece of cardboard pinned against it. He trod carefully towards the cabin, careful to move as quietly as possible. He gripped the gun tightly, a little amused that, in the event of anything serious happening, it would be absolutely useless, unless he shot someone in the eye, which would only temporarily slow them down. Maybe momentarily blind them. He hunkered down by the cabin, watching through the window. It was Eno, sitting up against the wall by the roaring fire only in his vest and trousers. He was completely still, legs splayed out, eyes staring blankly ahead. His intestines hung out of his stomach, a bloody unfinished gutting. A dark-haired woman crouched over him. A man's voice instructed her from the side. Sweat popped on Gill's forehead at the instant recognition. His chest caved in. Transfixed, he watched in horror as Bronwyn began eating Eno's intestines, scooping them in her hands, chewing, slurping and gorging. Only in her bra and fatigue trousers, she was covered with blue paint, her face smeared in it. Her hair was a tangled mess. Gill felt sick. He couldn't look away. His right leg began to twitch uncontrollably. He just about held up his body as Ziggy emerged from the shadows masturbating. His hand pumped up and down while Bronwyn continued to eat, snarling now as the fire crackled. Ziggy's ruggedly attractive face contorted in pleasure. He paused to take his trousers off, sank down. He grabbed Bronwyn by the hair dragging her towards him. She back-handed him. He laughed. Then she took his penis in her bloody mouth, head bobbing up and down as Ziggy groaned. Her tongue flicked, curled, licked. She sucked the moistened tip, the oozing translucent nectar. Ziggy leaned over to Eno, who'd had no idea his exit from this world would be a gruesome threesome to which he hadn't consented. He bit into Eno's shoulder, digging his teeth in, gnawing down into the bone just as he came in Bronwyn's mouth, just as she stained his come red. Her dark, cavernous mouth swallowed; the overgrown tongue licked her fingers. These were not the actions of bodies that were unfamiliar to each other. In agony, Gill stumbled backwards, an ache spreading through his chest intensely. He thought he'd shatter into pieces right there. He fell into an abyss littered with Ziggy and Bronwyn's shed skin. They broke the surface baring their teeth. Gill's heart rate increased. His nerves were frazzled. He couldn't breathe. He felt ill and delirious all at once. He retched violently, alerting them, steadying himself, hand gripping the window's edge. He dropped the gun. The door to the cabin flung open. He ran. He staggered blindly towards the brook, heavy with the knowledge of what he'd just seen, his body shaking in shock at the betrayal and Eno, deader than a zombie on a life-support machine, reduced to a kinky meal by the fire. God knew what they'd done with the other couples.

He heard rustling behind him, then ragged breathing, like a valve had been opened in his chest or thigh. Ziggy tackled him from behind, knocking the wind out of him. They fell into the brook, crashing down onto the angle where the night had upended into something warped and feral, its unruly mass unable to be measured by any known instrument. Hours before, they'd all been joking, laughing at the idea of adults playing games in the wilderness. Gill couldn't reconcile this with the change that had occurred in the space of several hours, like a rotten core beneath a silk cloth. Gill's head hit the rocks as he fell. Blood trickled down. Ziggy flew at him, punching him repeatedly, ferociously. As if he was a stranger, as if they didn't share a history, his knuckles raw from each hit, his eyes wild. 'I knew The Point would surprise you. People can't help being who they really are here, sooner or later,' he said, flexing his fingers, mouth twisted into a smile that was half grimace, half light.

'Fuck you. You're insane,' Gill said, struggling to breathe through his bloody nose, which felt pulverised. He tried to gather himself.

'Ah, well, it's all relative. In the spirit of transparency, I'm letting you know I'm going to get my gun, the real one. When I catch you, I'll kill you,' Ziggy warned.

'You'll have to catch me first, you cunt,' Gill spat, swiftly head-butting Ziggy three times with all the strength he could muster, catching him by surprise. Gill's head rang, shot through with pain from the impact. It was bitingly cold. His teeth chattered. His body was stiff, his knuckles bruised from the fall. He uncurled slowly, leaving Ziggy slightly dazed. If he wasn't injured, he was only just faster on foot than Ziggy. But Ziggy, he was certain, would know the area very well. It was just like him to have that advantage over the rest of them. Gill didn't know what lay beyond except more endless, sprawling wilderness. He figured his best bet was to go back the way he had come. He limped away, steadily started running. He didn't look behind.

They wanted him dead for the money, of course. He stood to inherit a cool fifteen million from his father's estate on the eve of his thirty-fifth birthday, six months away. The truth was, Gill had pushed it to the back of his mind for years, choosing to focus on his career instead, working hard to prove himself. In the event of his death, since he had no siblings, his wife would receive the money. Somehow he'd forgotten that Ziggy had been the one to introduce him to Bronwyn. Ziggy had known her first. How could he have forgotten that crucial detail? Something else bothered him, something that had been clawing at a block in his memory with gnarled fingers. Bile rose in his throat as realization dawned. He grabbed the photo from his pocket, shining the torchlight on the faces. It couldn't be.

The mascot.

The year they'd won the cup their mascot was a girl who'd trailed after him and Ziggy pathetically that season. They'd been cruel to her in the way guys that age can be.

But that girl had been mousy, awkward, buck-toothed. He stared at the mostly covered face. The nose was now different but the eyes were the same: cool emerald green. And Bronwyn was not naturally dark-haired. *Oh, God.* He'd known her before. He'd never really known her this time round. He dropped the torch, picked it up noting the small crack in the glass. He felt incapable of shouldering the weight he now carried, the burden of knowing what was unbearable. He felt small, vulnerable and inconsequential. The past incarnation of Bronwyn leaned against his head wound, its heartbeat growing stronger in the wild.

Gill arrived at the small smattering of cars before the main cabins with a bullet missing him by inches. Another grazed the Vauxhall Cavalier's bonnet. He fiddled for the car keys frantically. He noticed a body in the back seat. Ludwig: one side of his face had been eaten off. The passenger door wasn't properly closed. He didn't bother to shut it. His heart rate increased. He ran to the driver's side, dropped the keys accidentally. The cabins were witnesses whose lights had dimmed, who kept their secrets firmly locked inside. Gill was frozen by this stage, trembling uncontrollably again. He could barely move his limbs. He'd got lost twice on the way back, which hadn't helped. At one point he'd started howling from the pain of it all, the deep, fractured sound a marauding vibration with its own will. He'd spun around abruptly, paranoid, so out of his mind he worried his gun had somehow caught up with him, that the sound was coming from it, not him. He heard Ziggy singing the line *my sweetheart come along!*, Bronwyn snarling, getting closer. He remembered how she'd given him a cooked artichoke on their wedding night, then told him to attempt feeding its chopped heart to an eel on one of his studies. He remembered thinking it was an odd thing to suggest. Her response had been that people should submit to the incongruous sides of themselves more often, that if you ate something enough without judgement, you could develop a taste for it. He'd dropped the artichoke heart into the Thames, watching as if the darkened current had spawned it before it scattered.

Staying low, Gill dived inside the car, switched the engine on, listening in case it started not just the vehicle but the body in the back. He hit the accelerator. The body slid down, dangling halfway out of the open door. He tore off onto the roads. He glanced at the rear-view mirror. They were chasing him. Ziggy held the gun in one hand. Bronwyn was in a contraption similar to a baby harness and reins. *Jesus.*

Her bra was off, her nipples perked, blood dribbled down her chin. Tears ran down Gill's cheeks. He didn't recognise this woman or his friend. This woman, to whose dip in the back he'd confessed his greatest fears while she snoozed, whose waist he'd imagined expanding as they got older, that he'd enjoy it and still curve his hand there. And still consider it a place of solace to breathe against because it had been, to dampen with his tongue watching for its turns in half-lights, in the traffic of intimate bodies. And because that was some kind of joy he'd never fully understood until now.

He was faint from the head injury, from the loss. He looked at the rear-view mirror again, they were gaining on him. Impossible. He shifted the car into fifth gear. The road splintered, the mountains became quiet, shrinking mounds, the coming dawn their god. Now Ziggy and Bronwyn were fluttering in the side mirrors, shrieking, biting down on the bone again, sucking the marrow from everything he'd thought he knew. Gill felt something drop from his insides. As if a vacuum of air had swallowed his organs. Everything went dark. His head hit the wheel. His foot slackened on the accelerator. The moon had stopped leaking. The jaws of an intersection between the night and the morning opened, having bred them for a reckoning.

The sign for *Coetiroedd Ymadael* vanished.

Grace Jones

Once the stray parts of a singed scene had found their way into the bedroom, onyx edges gleaming and the figures without memories had lost their molten heads to the coming morning, after she'd pressed her face against the space under the doorway crying, reaching for some untouched handful of earth as sustenance, the agency called, Hassan more specifically. She'd narrowed down the thing she planned to do that day to three options, stark, cold and clinical, on a creased receipt for a disco-light-hued Roland Mouret jacket she'd worn only once. But the phone rang, shrill, invasive, demanding. Still on the floor, the wood cold against her skin, she crawled to the receiver tentatively, as if her limbs were tethered to a thread on the earth's equator, the thread bending and collapsing into the different stages of her life. She contemplated the ways she could delay each inevitable outcome on the receipt. She could swallow it, wait for its disintegration in her stomach, acid eroding the words into nothing. She could shit it out.

Could you shit out paper? That would particularly encapsulate what it was: ugly. Or she could simply misplace it in the flat somewhere. Not outside. Definitely not outside. It would be gone for ever then. She'd have to go through options again, add new ones, whittle it down. That process had left her brain frazzled overnight, her heart leaking through the bedroom keyhole, making a sucking sound as her hands turned to wax. The receipt would have to be misplaced indoors. That would give her the option of attempting to stretch the boundaries of time despite an internal wound the shape of a turret. In her mind, the draughtsman was God. He had placed the turret inside her chest. Earlier, he'd drawn her in various angles, electric blue lines delivering degrees of shock from the same incident. Each time she got up. Each time she felt the weight of the turret tumbling in the ether.

She picked up the receiver, cradled it firmly, careful not to let it slip from her grasp the way things had of late. For a few seconds there was silence at the other end. She knew it was Hassan. He usually waited several beats before speaking, as if allowing you time to adjust to a different frequency. He never introduced himself. He just expected you to know. And she always did.

Sidra, so there's a party tonight. You don't have to attend, might be fun, though. The guy's a big Grace Jones fan. I've texted you the address. Do what you do. Any problems, call me. Cool?

Bet.

She almost told him about the draughtsman then. She found herself wanting to do it at the most unexpected times. Instead she put the receiver down, hands trembling.

She checked the table for the receipt. It had fallen onto the floor by the radiator, already misplacing itself. She'd forgotten to tell Hassan that she was considering taking an evening class one day a week. They were like that, so many things constantly left unsaid. She'd never asked him what a French Algerian man was doing running a lookalike agency in London among other things. And he'd never asked what a girl from Martinique with a degree in forensics was doing moonlighting as a Grace Jones impersonator, the translated versions of themselves staring at each other silently from the opposite sides of a revolving door.

There was a building that remained a husk; a blackened, charcoaled carcass gutted from the inside out. The carcass leaned against the heavens in protest at its losses, at its snatched internal sky tainted with the fingerprints of one last daily procession, rituals of the living. And while the world slept, awoke, the cities hummed with chaos and order; rivers began in cotton pockets cupping slackened fists; the waters undulated into lost reflections; the gods got high off the colours from the seas; the equator adjusted itself only slightly; the stars twinkled in haphazard collusion; the mountains dappled by hammer tan winds that became personal directions; the building remained, an artificial gut bathed in degrees of light, lodged in the stages of a day. The building was a hollow within a carcass within a husk within a world within a galaxy; a series of crooked boxes varying in size inside each other where the gift was always the same, always attached to a bottom that had gone missing. On each floor of the husk, Sidra was running backwards to the late afternoon of a day. It had been flat-packed into cardboard boxes sealed with Sellotape. On each floor Sidra peeled off the Sellotape, the sound a split in the air whose line couldn't be traced. She removed items from the box. The late afternoon that day was made up of ingredients for cake: eggs, flour, butter, sugar, tinfoil, a whisk, vanilla.

On each floor Sidra ran to the window where she stood in costumes made of tinfoil.

On floor one she was covered with eggs, screaming.

On floor two she was drenched in flour, howling.

On floor three she was soaked in butter, melting as a heat intensified while the whisk whirred ominously on the periphery.

And so on.

Grace Jones's 'La Vie en Rose' played on a radio that wasn't plugged in anywhere. Instead the plug sprang from the bottom of the building, like an untethered electrical root.

The husk shook.

On each floor Sidra grabbed the whisk. Lost scenes fell out from the windows; water was inadequate. Hoses throbbed with adrenalin and burned hearts; death traps, the lifts became stuck all over again spewing firemen's costumes like

*overgrown fabricated insects. Like genesis on speed, everything
escalated quickly. Ashes assembled into figures crawling on the
skyline before colliding with traffic, which destroyed them all
over again.*

    The equator turned a fraction.

    The flames rose.

    The bottoms of the crooked boxes were set alight.

    Debris became glowing cinders that walked.

    A dot appeared on the galaxy.

    *The draughtsman held a flame he angled like a stick of lead,
like a tool that could change guise at any point.*

Sidra had first seen Grace on TV. She must have been
around thirteen at the time. She'd been chasing Carla and
Dorian, who were playing with a set of screwdrivers behind
the sofa, darting forwards and backwards in a mock game
of fencing, shouting, '*En garde!*' sporadically, brandishing
the screwdrivers like long, elegantly carved swords. The
washing-machine was spinning. The windows were open to
hide evidence of her botched attempt at gumbo. The smoke
alarm was broken. Half an hour earlier, it had beeped incessantly. In her frustrated efforts to silence it, she'd broken it
with a broom. But none of that mattered because a woman
who looked like her was on TV. Pulled to the screen by an
instinct she didn't quite understand, she stared. It was on
BBC1. She'd never seen a black woman so unapologetically
dark on the screen. It was beautiful and she was hypnotised.

Dressed in an all-black cat suit, the woman was tall, striking, other-worldly, confident.

Her mouth painted fire-engine red, her head was in an off-yellow helmet shaped like a bees' nest. Sidra half expected a swarm of bees to hover over the woman's head, the queen bee in action. She felt as if they'd shared the same womb, separated by a few decades and a trail of bees' fat with mutual DNA and womb lining.

Grace Jones, they said. *Grace Jones.*

She repeated the words aloud, feeling them roll off her tongue while the washing-machine spun, while Carla and Dorian swapped the screwdrivers for Power Ranger toys starting wars in patois. The screen jumped, flickered, the picture vanished.

Grace had been brought to her on a signal from Jupiter. She grabbed the hanger on the floor behind the TV, stretched its curved head and inserted it into the television's aerial socket. The picture returned. Grace was gone, replaced by an item on an infected brand of milk. Her heart sank but the image of Grace was burned into her head as if with an iron. She ran to her mother's room, opened her make-up drawers searching through the lipsticks, pouting her lips. She flung the wardrobe door open, its mirrors multiplying her automatically. She dived in. In the dark, she heard the flutter of a wing. A bee with a fire-engine-red mouth floated in a trail of static.

*

Sidra hopped into a cab to East Dulwich, the Roland Mouret jacket shimmering in the cold night. Her Yves St Laurent perfume mingled with a scent that smelt oddly like pot-pourri. Her red velvet backless cat suit was warm and luxurious against her skin. In the back seat, she could make out the top of her face in the rear-view mirror: short back and sides, no fuss, good to go. Dangling from the mirror was a miniature golden Aladdin-esque lamp. She sank into the seat as the city unfolded, fingers tracing the possibilities of the inky darkness, picturing the lamp spilling petrol into the hemline of a dress she'd decided not to wear. She rolled the window down as the driver talked non-stop about being a boy in Damascus. The cool breeze pricked her skin. She closed her eyes, the driver's ramblings seeping in almost subconsciously.

She hadn't been to East Dulwich for a few years. Not since she'd worked for a mobile massage company for one week. That first job, she'd found a slender, bespectacled man of average height sprinkling the green outside a large house in a silk kimono-style dressing-gown. He adjusted the wire-rimmed glasses perched on his nose intermittently as if out of habit. The house was like something from *Wallpaper* magazine: futuristic, slightly incongruous in that leafy, suburban street. He abandoned the sprinkler, pleased at the sight of her, motioned towards the open front door. They walked in. In the hallway, he disappeared for roughly a minute, then reappeared holding a towel.

He handed her the towel, instructing her to change in the downstairs bathroom ahead, £150 for a topless forty-minute massage.

She got ready. Dressed in black panties, netted stockings, suspenders and a silver cape she climbed the stairs where she found him in a neon wrestling outfit in the master bedroom, a pot of cream standing on a lovingly crafted small bedside table. They wrestled for ten minutes. Then she smeared the cream on his face, yanking his head down into the puddle of white on the wooden floor, forcing him to lick it.

Afterwards, stripped down on the bed, the light fracturing on the chandelier, she kneaded his hairy back. He groaned, complimenting the warmth of her hands.

The fire for him started in the bathroom with the draughtsman sitting at the edge of the tub wearing her silver cape, smiling encouragingly.

That week, the fires began in a different room each time: a basement, a study, a conservatory. Sidra would always remember that first one: the silken kimono flapping open to reveal an expanse of thigh, a line of hair creeping into his groin, the cuckoo clock with a tiny woman whose arms were the hands of time, whose cuckooing mouth was decorated with soot that would spread, the irony of the sprinkler still turning on the green as she left, watering kernels of afternoon secrets before lapsing into silence.

*

The cab pulled up to a Georgian mansion. Sidra paid, tipping the driver an extra ten pounds for his stories. She jumped out, crossing the large stretch of lawn dotted with pale tents draped with flickering lights, a hedge carved into the shape of a figure holding a chainsaw and a life-sized family of ice swans craning their necks towards each other, slowly thawing into the grass. She knocked on the door. A Marilyn Monroe lookalike opened it, appropriately dressed in a bombshell blue polka-dot sixties dress.

'Welcome!' she announced theatrically. 'You look fabulous,' she added, stepping aside to allow Sidra entrance. The waft of warm air smelt like expensive aftershaves, mince pies, perfume. The décor was classily understated, with colourful touches here and there. Sidra raised her head. There were three floors, from what she could see. Bodies everywhere, jostling, sliding and wriggling through as if they'd been let out of giant tin cans slick and oiled in some saccharine sheen for excess, the sharp, opened-can ceilings edging closely to their foreheads as they moved. She took off her jacket, slipping it over her arm as a Rod Stewart lookalike approached, offering to take it. She declined, looking beyond him to a tray of hors d'oeuvres being served by a Pee-wee Herman lookalike in a grey suit, white brogues, topped off with a red bow tie. She assessed the guests. There were no other black people. She wasn't planning on serving any hors d'oeuvres. *Fuck that shit.* She was used to being the only black female lookalike at this sort of gathering unless Tina Turner showed up, cutting her out of oxygen and attention. Tina wasn't there. Thank God.

Marilyn Monroe had smoothly grabbed her a glass of white wine. She took the hollow-stemmed flute. 'You look so much like her,' Sidra said, offering what every impersonator wanted to hear.

Marilyn blushed. 'My heart just jumped with joy,' she answered breathlessly, in a perfect impersonation of her idol. 'Luigi's just through in the other room.'

Sidra followed the sound of the piano to Luigi, their host, a squat, balding, jewelled, enthusiastic film producer, who made the phrase 'larger than life' inadequate in his presence. Celebrating his annual end-of-year soirée, he sat before a sleek black piano, flanked by three Venuses feeding him miniature salmon slices topped with cream on tiny puffs of pastry. Delighted, Luigi pointed at her. 'Pull up to my bumper, baby!' He bashed the piano keys dramatically. A crowd circled her. Sidra tugged her handbag strap up her shoulder. The small crowd were gasping, barely restraining themselves from reaching out to touch her, chattering over each other.

She smiled at this part of what was essentially a ceremony, a performance. This part always felt good. The bodies leaned in, clutching their wine glasses. The draughtsman appeared behind them holding two yellow-handled screwdrivers. There were tongues in the wine flutes, floating, then curling mid-scream, sinking to the bottom. Sidra closed her eyes momentarily as the humming in her brain began. She disappeared into her role: Grace Jones.

Several months back, there'd been another party, a masked ball in Paris in a former museum on the border of the Champs-Élysées. There on business, Hassan had informed her he might or might not attend. He was elusive that way. She never knew when he'd turn up to keep a distant but watchful eye on events. As the owner of the agency he didn't need to; occasionally he materialised to keep his band of impersonators on their toes.

She'd left the mingling crowds, making her way through a maze of decadent rooms until she entered one right at the back of the building. Original surrealist paintings hung on the walls, tanks full of moon starfish slowly pulsed rhythmically in calm, contained, lit waters. A deep Egyptian gold-trimmed coffin lay open. She'd been running her fingers over the trimming when she felt a hand on her back, a finger slowly circling. Something about that touch felt familiar. She leaned into it, ill-equipped to resist an unspooling occurring in her stomach.

'Hassan?' She turned around. The man didn't speak. He wore an intricately designed silver mask. There was no way to make out his face. Dressed in an exquisitely tailored midnight-blue suit, which complemented his skin tone, he reminded her of Hassan. He was similar in height, stature, tall and lean, possibly Arab. He had the same unruly head of curly hair. A smell like Cuban cigars and spirit-lined edges emanated from him. He possessed the same amused glint in his eyes. Instead of answering her, he took her hand, led her into the silk-lined coffin. He reached under her bulbous terracotta-coloured ballgown skirt, took off her panties. He parted her arse, burying his tongue there, licking and sucking greedily, groaning as his tongue circled, darted and fucked her rectum as though it was an edible orchid. He fucked her in that coffin without taking off a stitch of clothing. They were realigned, cushioned by folds of material. Sidra revealed her secret as she came, unable to understand how it had emerged from a burrow within her. He didn't react, as if he hadn't heard her. Stepping out of the coffin, their silence was a shared language. He kissed her neck tenderly before leaving. The moon starfish exited their tanks, floated towards her, running out of time.

Back in the main space, she scanned the crowds dribbling in different directions. He'd vanished. She headed outside to catch her breath in the courtyard. The moon starfish became mushrooms falling from her skin.

Three weeks later in London, Hassan invited her to a working-lunch meeting. He was immaculate, of course, in a teak-coloured Ozwald Boateng blazer, black polo neck and slacks. He had a way of making instructions sound like casual suggestions, though with an undertone that made it clear he was absolutely serious. In between his briefing, she caught an unexpected expression on his face.

She'd been reaching into her purse to pay half of the bill. He was watching her as if he knew her intimately. It was a warm, mischievous look, so fleeting that afterwards she thought she'd imagined it. Then, his eyes became hooded, his expression darkened. 'It's an easy gig. No matter how inebriated you get, avoid leaving with anybody you don't know. I don't want a fucking heart attack in my mid-thirties. And stay away from stuff with traces of peanut. You're allergic. Remember that time your face swelled up? You looked like the Elephant Woman.' He chuckled.

Sidra cringed internally at the memory. Of course he'd remember that embarrassing incident. He told her about his trip to Greece, his work providing for and coordinating the refugee relief there. He spoke passionately at some length, relaying amusing tales fondly of some of the characters he'd encountered, the children in particular, how crazy the camps were, the camaraderie formed despite the desperation of their situation. She hadn't expected that level of generosity from him. The truth was, she knew very little about him beyond their working relationship. She suspected even his occasional revelations were calculated, though she was unsure as to what end.

'Is there something you'd like to tell me?' he asked. 'Anything you're unhappy about work-wise?' he nudged gently.

One hand in her purse, Sidra held the perfume bottle. The draughtsman materialised, standing beside Hassan with smoke curling from his clothes. His drawing instruments were snapped in his hands. Sidra's fingers trembled.

'I have to go.' She stood abruptly, knocking a plate containing the last remnants of an omelette. She started grabbing cash from her purse. Hassan scowled.

She put the purse down.

Marilyn Monroe sashayed by holding a tray of diced blue cheese. Sidra grabbed a piece by the staircase, popping it into her mouth; she savoured the taste to submerge the sick feeling rising in her stomach.

The fire that started it all had been an accident, so she'd been told. That day, her mother Marianne, having swapped shifts with a colleague, returned to their flat late afternoon. Often misplacing her keys, she'd rung the buzzer, kissed them, briefly admonished Carla and Dorian for the puzzle pieces of Ninja Turtles strewn on the hallway floor, passing Sidra in the kitchen rummaging through the cupboards, ingredients laid out on the table. 'Hope we're having more than cake for dinner,' she said, smiling, before peeling off her nursing uniform then crawling into bed. At the kitchen table, Sidra scribbled down a brief list. They'd run out of vanilla extract, the flour wasn't enough, no icing sugar left. She slipped on her jacket, trainers. She double-locked the flat door with her keys, as she often did if she needed to pop out, briefly leaving her siblings alone. The lift smelt of piss and sweat, groaning all the way down fourteen floors, shuddering as if it would spit her out onto an exit beyond the confines of the building. She departed it, remembering she'd knocked the roll of tinfoil onto the kitchen floor, left the fridge and cupboard doors open, Carla and Dorian arguing about a broken toy plane. She'd recall those details later. She'd weigh them in her hands, wrap them in tinfoil, pass them through the expanding hole in her chest, watching their arrival on a periphery, bloody, misshapen, despite their thin veil of protection.

It was the vanilla extract that delayed her. They'd run out of it practically everywhere in their area. She'd had to walk all the way down to the cash-and-carry at the end of the main road to find a bottle. Forty minutes was all it took to lose everything. She arrived back to find their block engulfed in flames. The fire was ferocious. People jumped out of windows from the lower floors; babies were thrown out in duvets; bed sheets were used as inadequate ropes. The popping of fire, the screams of panic strangled her internally. She spilled the shopping on the horizon, the icing darkened by a trail of soot, the vanilla bottle breathing smoke, the flour dousing trees, windows, hands on car wheels steering, fingers jamming in ignitions instead of keys. It didn't matter which element of the scene she stumbled on unexpectedly, her mother, Carla and Dorian were trapped. The fire raged on. Her brother and sister died in their mother's arms. Powerless, Sidra had stood on the pavement looking up, screaming, a chipped chess piece floundering between the firemen, hoses, the crowd.

She'd locked her family in to protect them. She'd locked her family in, killing them.

The parts of that memory always assembled into the same inevitable ending.

She'd brought out the keys, her hands shaking uncontrollably, her mouth babbling mother, cake, fridge, lift, uniform. She tried inserting the keys inside their names as if they were locks that would open, materialise them in her arms so she could breathe again. Instead the keys stuck, refusing to turn. They jammed in every opening, every possibility of rescue. In the years that were to follow, Sidra would encounter her actions that day again and again. And the draughtsman started appearing.

The party continued, a barely contained beast sprouting various heads while the skyline unfurled. Pee-wee Herman knelt in the garden doorway drinking Dom Pérignon from another man's shoes. Luigi had disappeared from his own celebration. A silver-haired contortionist lay sprawled atop the piano, twisting, then curling her body into astonishing shapes as bright ties spilled from her mouth. People were doing lines of coke on the staircase, in the toilets, on the pantry floor. In the ground-floor bathroom there were bodies in the tub, clothed mannequins blinking at the harsh light, knocked out by their debauchery and excess. There were people fucking in the tents on the lawn, the cold air mottling their skin, the small decorative lights jangling as if indicating the tents might collapse, folding into bodies as part of the thrill.

Inside the kitchen, Sidra thought about the sharp instruments that found their way into the margins of her life, how they blunted against her body. She reached for a plum from a bowl of fruit on the grey marble island top. Instead of cores, in her mind's eye the fruit had miniature blackened vanilla-extract bottles spilling elixir for multiple deaths. She held up the plum. The draughtsman took a bite. She glanced at the hallway. There were bodies all the way up the banister shedding alligator skin, mouths holding their vices between knocked-out teeth, feet leaking watery reflections. The draughtsman finished the plum. Sidra took another swig of wine, looked up at the patterns of swirls on the white ceiling, longing for some entity to pull her through rust, wood, metal, bone, perform an excavation that would leave her changed. She felt hollow, gutted. She'd become acclimatised to scenes of this nature, adjusting herself in degrees, like a heating dial.

Before the tower block became a burned husk there stood an old print house in its place. Before the print house there were raw materials to build it. Before those raw materials there was a draughtsman named Alrik, armed with a vision. Before the vision there was a perilous journey crossing the Atlantic Ocean to England by ship. Alrik had left behind a young son and a spirited wife, whose plans to join him in London spurred him on while he searched for work. But his wife and son died of cholera making that same journey, which for him had been loaded with hunger, curiosity and wonder at the potential of his new life. Their bodies were flung into the cold, thrashing sea. Broken-hearted and forlorn, Alrik spent time numbing his loss in the opium dens of London. It was in one such den that the image of the print house came to him, a building where men printed endless trails of paper, a building topped off with a turret, a kind of signature, a reference to his travels beyond the Americas. The image was ingrained in his memory that night at the den in Limehouse, floating alluringly between curls of smoke. Roughly a month later, Alrik got himself a job at a construction company. He worked his way up. By the time the print house was built in 1920, he'd married a grocer's daughter named Bethany. They had three sons. He went on to draft designs for other projects but the print house remained his favourite because it came to him during a period of great pain, its lines somehow made indelible in his bloodstream, constructed in memory of his first wife and son.

Before he died, Alrik was grateful the building would outlive him. In 1970, his beautiful print house was knocked down, having been a barely used museum for years, and replaced by an ugly tower block of flats. Resurrected from the rubble, Alrik began to wander through the tower block regularly. He entered people's flats, breathed against oven doors, sources of electricity. He searched for his departed reflection in their mirrors. Resentful, angry, he set small accidents for which occupants would absentmindedly feel responsible. Dissatisfied, over the years he began to plot a bigger accident worthy of his loss. At first, he simply fiddled with the wiring of the building, ensured the lifts malfunctioned now and again, and removed the fire extinguishers. Over time, his acts of malice grew. The draughtsman cultivated his appetite for destruction.

Sidra had met the real Grace Jones once after her concert at the Royal Albert Hall, for which Grace had been fashionably an hour late. She'd cornered her at the end by the backstage entrance, fighting through other bodies jostling to do the same.

'Grace!' she'd hollered, overwhelmed by excitement. 'People tell me I remind them of you.'

Grace, decked in a tight see-through chiffon dress, purple knee-length boots and white three-D glasses smiled patiently, tolerantly. 'Dahhhling, imitation is for pagans but you are divine.'

Sidra found Luigi strangling one of the Venuses in the secret garden behind an initial smaller, more standard-looking garden. It ran lengthways. Venus was so out of it, she could barely fight back or scream. Her feet kicked limply. Her soiled, sequined dress's train was a fish tail moored on the wrong Garden of Eden. A little unsteadily, Sidra set her jacket down. She leaped onto Luigi pummelling his back. 'Leave her alone!'

Venus's underwear was gone; there were bruises already forming on her thighs. For a rotund, shorter man, Luigi was surprisingly strong. Barely recognisable as the charming host she'd encountered several hours earlier, he wore a chilling, cold expression. 'Fuck off, you cunt.' Turning around, he punched Sidra in the face repeatedly. Venus stared blankly at a night sky that wouldn't rescue her. Sidra fell backwards. The wind left her body. Her head spun; her handbag went flying. She felt the weight of the perfume bottle slide as it moved. Blood trickled from her nose into her mouth. Her face throbbed. She looked at her Roland Mouret jacket, half expecting it to morph into a parachute, a dizzying, shimmering distraction from the ache in her head, which felt like it would fracture. Then, there were four other Grace Jones lookalikes dressed exactly like her. They all reached for her purse, for an item that accompanied her constantly: petrol in a perfume bottle, a beating heart liquefied.

The draughtsman resurfaced and all his fingers were flames.

The fire at Luigi's was voracious. Just like all the others. It swallowed the once-glorious building, tore through the roof. It puffed black smoke, spat screaming bodies out. On the front lawn, Sidra coughed from the smoke in her lungs. Luigi, engulfed in flames, ran erratically, a wind-up life-sized toy, attempting to put himself out.

The pale tents empty of bodies were on fire; the ice swans' heads had melted, the remains of their figures thinning mockingly; the giant hedge man had lost his chainsaw. Ambulance and fire engine sirens screamed in the distance.

A familiar figure ran towards her. Hassan. He looked dishevelled, half panicked, a tight expression on his face. This man who was always cool, calm and assured grabbed her in relief. 'Thank God! This was on the news. I was out of my mind with worry. You're going to give me internal injuries before I hit forty.' He cupped her battered face. 'Who did this? I'll kill him.'

She tried to speak but couldn't. What she wanted to say was: Couldn't somebody hear her silently screaming inside for years? Couldn't somebody in this fucking world get their hands bloody reaching into her guts to find something jagged and beautiful she could hold up to the light? Couldn't somebody see that she disappeared into Grace Jones because the pain, the guilt, the loneliness of being herself was unbearable? Couldn't somebody remind her of her favourite thing about being alive since she'd forgotten? Couldn't somebody find the bright yolk she'd lost in the back of a cab on a rainy afternoon, then present it to her as a new beginning? Couldn't somebody just be tender?

She stuck her hand into her jacket pocket. A receipt poked out; it fell. She hadn't remembered slipping it in there but she must have done. Miraculously, it had survived the fire. She'd taken the inside creature outside, disguised as a creased receipt. She wondered if it would anger the draughtsman. Hassan held the receipt, gazing at the three options she'd written down. Shaken, he stared as if holding a grenade pin with the world attached to it. He ripped up the receipt, its pieces fluttering in the cold air as the fire raged behind them.

'When you're ready, tell me what you've been scared to say,' he suggested. She started crying then. He held her, pressed his mouth against the pulse in her neck as if it was a light travelling, as if it would be mercury by the time he finished knowing it. He held onto her. They braced themselves for the weather in the cracks, for the draughtsman's next stroke.

Saudade Minus One (S–1 =)

After being left at their pick-up points, the boys from Batch 2 of the US government's Camp Omega training unit felt the echoes of choppers shrinking to a quiet blue line inside them. All the same age – thirteen – they were dropped off in the latest cycle. Six boys deposited in the forgotten towns of Midwestern America one by one, on a bridge, an underpass or in an abandoned building used as a bleak refuge in the night, where the gargoyles of the city patiently watched for something golden amid soiled mattresses, gutted cars, upturned rotted fridges.

Every Batch 2 boy held a catapult. Waiting, their hands clung to their familiar reassurance.

On that morning, in that unnamed town, Elmira headed out to meet her new son. The sky was having an asthma attack manifesting as mist. She knew this would trigger her own attack but couldn't predict when it would happen. She never could. As she left the ranch she steadied her nerves, and trembling, calloused hands, by rubbing them against the loose blue beads in her pocket she'd collected from a vision of a cornfield of sons strangling their mothers. They were small, miscoloured planets gathering momentum in their cotton gateway.

Her pick-up point was the bridge over the river, decayed and moss-covered at the ends. En route, she passed the empty gas station where the coyotes didn't even bother waiting till evening before making appearances. They gathered in clusters like a small, infected travelling colony. Some were greedily licking the nozzles of long dried pumps, others prowling the counter, hopping on and off with stained dollar notes between their teeth, others taking turns to sit on freezers that stored the hum of long-gone car engines. The coyotes prowled with the sounds of ignitions in their chests, like second heartbeats.

Elmira passed a white church as its thick wooden door swung open from a gust of wind. She looked up. A hologram sat on the rooftop smoking a blueprint, holding a wailing cow's mouth in her other hand. She passed the school with no children, tempted by its rusted black gates, pushing them back to feel their weight, as if that one action would release old scenes through the bars: a boy ripping the pages of an exercise book into the shape of a crow that didn't leave his Achilles heel; a girl whose breakfast consisted of slim pieces of chalk reduced to white dust in her chest; the pockmark-faced, nicotine-breathing maths tutor, who slyly taught Hungarian to children who mimicked his mutterings at their dinner tables: *Hibas! Termeszetellenes, Nines Isten!* Elmira left the gate containing its equally rusted memories.

She arrived at the bridge sooner than anticipated, knowing it was her desire to escape memories that caught her unaware in spaces that always deceived.

Her new son stood fiddling with his catapult on the bridge, the mist curling slowly to reveal him, as if he'd been born to her thirteen years old, through a gap in the sky. Elmira couldn't help assessing how he'd feel in her arms, how many injuries he might accumulate during their time together, whether she'd be able to sketch them at night, if they'd sneakily reappear as visions in the days before they fully healed. She couldn't stop her heartbeat quickening, or her mouth slowly gathering mist like a new form of breathing. She abruptly pulled her hand from the pocket of her long black cotton skirt and a few beads spilled out. She dived to the ground, panicked at the thought of losing them before her son.

This was their introduction, she scrambling after the beads, and the blue-eyed, auburn-haired, solemn-looking boy slowly raising his left arm, the letter and numeral B2 imprinted on it.

She wondered how long he'd been standing in the cold, the catapult in his left hand smacking against his thigh repeatedly at the same speed and angle. He was dressed in dark, ill-fitting clothes that didn't belong to him. She knew this by the way the navy shirt hung off him, by the slight bagginess of the fatigue trousers. She spotted the Omega emblem of a small tank on his left sleeve. She made a note mentally to check the government had paid the fee of three thousand dollars into her account for fostering him. Elmira wanted to say she had other clothes stored in her barn she thought might fit him. Clothes she laid out for parts of her visions to try on, only for them to find them inadequate and fold them away beneath bales of hay in case she wanted to feed them to her vision of the snorting bull falling from the lines of the roof. A split, hungry creature identified after it passed through fleetingly.

As she approached, he deftly stilled the catapult, an action practised at intersections just like this for hollowed women like her with the same intent. A man, his face weathered, passed, pushing a wheelbarrow of potatoes and engine parts. His hands were greasy. The squeaky wheel-barrow was a welcome distraction.

Elmira felt a heightened sense of her surroundings, and was struck by visions. Of the bridge being a stony path suspended beneath a changeable sky, which coughed up these images of exchange. Of reward and half-formed devastations softened by murky rain. The boy shoved the catapult into his left pocket. The strap dangled out, not quite fitting. She worried her beads would spill again to meet the strap halfway. As if that action of unspooling would be her early inheritance for him. The boy's forehead wrinkled. She was almost in his physical space now, imagining things being trapped inside his expression; a curl of smoke needing to get to a small fire, the last line of an anthem.

'What will you call me?' the boy asked.

'What name would you like?' Elmira was surprised by the sound of her voice. It was thin, cracked by the weight of expectation carried since early that morning.

'I like Houdini,' he answered, deadly serious. 'It's good for a boy like me.'

There was a flicker in his face, not quite sadness but the look of someone resigned to their fate. Bulbs of cold sweat appeared on Elmira's forehead. The river beneath them shimmered with the wayward angles of days to come, with the shapes of items caught in nets wrestling stray tides. Elmira thought of the night she had waded into the river fully clothed, clutching two coyote heads, trying to press their eyes against the moon. An impossible task, the heads had cried. She had left them in the water to travel, reappear as presents for somebody less fortunate than her. Afterwards, she dropped her wet clothes in the barn to dry. She ate beetroot naked at the kitchen table until she knew her tongue had changed colour.

'Houdini will do,' she responded finally, noting the azure colour of his eyes. 'What about the other boys in Batch Two? Did you know them?'

He nodded, watching her carefully as if she'd shrunk and he'd caught her in a tall tumbler trying to break the glass with her breath. 'We made catapults together. We did tasks to test memory capacity. They, too, have been dispatched.'

They, too, have been dispatched. She smiled. It was a funny sentence from a young boy. She tasted beetroot and coyote tears and pictured the boys of Batch 2 falling between the spaces of those words, landing in empty buildings and derelict factories, talking with the countenance of adults to strange, parched women they would temporarily call mother.

She checked his head for patches of anything unusual, then ran her fingers over his teeth, rubbing the jagged molars on either side as though they'd reveal something.

He stuck out his tongue for inspection. She was relieved it didn't bear the blue stamp of a child damaged from too many cycles. She'd seen first-hand how such a child could malfunction in a new environment: the deadened eyes, an unwillingness to follow instructions, a regression in their training. She'd spotted a damaged child once, on one of the back roads of the town, repeatedly slamming an abandoned Buick door against his left hand, only screaming roughly two minutes later, a delayed reaction. She'd wondered how many delayed reactions he'd had, how often they'd occurred, the possibility of measuring their timings as if that would have changed anything. Then he'd picked up a metal bar, smashing it on the car at a speed and rate that would have been impressive had such an endeavour been a sport. The boy unleashed the algorithm of destruction. The windscreen shattered. The boy didn't stop. That was a different time. She hadn't been able to control parts of her visions then, or the pain that racked her body from a cycle coming to an end.

The flame-haired boy who stood before her now, calmly watching her movements, was not that boy. This was a boy from Batch 2, which she interpreted as progression, an advancement in training and ability. Less scope for malfunction. She imagined him misdirecting the feelings of belonging from a past cycle into the ether, speckled with shattered windscreen glass.

She said, 'Last winter three of my cows died from something in the river that transfixed them. They drank it. I think it's out again, loose on the ranch.' She rubbed her beads.

A flicker of a shadow passed over his eyes. 'I have the same dream of a dog chasing a yolk. The dog always wins.' He stared at her blankly. Repetition, an algorithm that diverted panic. She stopped rubbing her beads, somehow reassured. The boy was solemn, melancholy even, but she never could stand happy, boisterous children. Too much energy, too much optimism waiting to be broken down the line. His dreaming of dogs and yolks at night and her visions in the day meant they had something in common. Only she didn't know what it was yet.

*

That first evening at the ranch, Houdini discovered it was a home for stillborns brought to life with technology that didn't grow past the age of one. They were Elmira's stillborns. She had allowed them to be experimented on as part of the government's Llewellyn programme, which saw dead babies brought to life or live ones modified with mechanical parts, a combination of nature and scientific engineering. It was a grim way to save the ranch, money for small horrors who weren't definitively human. The residue of these experiments was kept at the far end of the barn: four large copper tanks, a broken operating table, rusted medical instruments in large jars, and several dark green Yugoslavian gas masks dotted around, like uninvited guests. The stillborns' irises were bright blue. Thick black wires sprang from their genitals, like artificial umbilical cords. Their partially collapsed heads contained small rectangular silver chips. Their remotely controlled mouths slackened unexpectedly, opening and closing to reveal miniature pits of darkness with teeth, but no tongue, sparking in the night. They hollered when he tried to pick them up, their small, concave chests housing circuit boards. He counted nine of them. Nine babies who technically shouldn't have existed. They were pulled to him by a silent undertow slipping between their limbs. They crawled up his legs, clutching handfuls of soil as offerings, and circled each other on the wooden floor of his room. It was a plain affair with only a creaky single mattress and a lamplight on the dresser next to Elmira's sketches of Noah's Ark, a vision within a vision, two of each animal.

He put three of the babies to sleep in the barn, perched on top of bales of hay and clothing they'd never grow into. The babies blinked up at him, chewing on electrical umbilical cords. The other six he placed in the large, empty copper water tank.

He stood watching their movements for several moments, the slow bending of their wires. He began to make the sound of gunshots, frightening them, remembering that Elmira had divulged she'd been feeding them pesticides. He increased the volume of the shots. The babies started wailing; the three fell off the bales of hay, landing on their backs, fists opening and closing. The ones in the tank began to smack their heads against it, eyes fully red. Houdini approached the tank. He placed his hand inside. One baby bit him. He filed each image away. He raised his arm up slowly to the light, watching for an injury that wasn't there.

The morning of their first full day together was bright, loaded with promise and sunshine. The ranch was a contained ramshackle kingdom, spilling living stillborns from its cracks. The white patterns of planes in the sky drifted down to the empty pigsty. The soil smelt damp and earthy from a few days of rain.

Houdini's first task was to milk the restless cows. Elmira accompanied him, holding a small metallic bucket. Thick, dark Afro curls whipped about her lean, toffee-hued face. A faint line of moustache graced her top lip. Her dimpled smile, when revealed, was infectious. She was beautiful, possessing the demeanour of a woman who had far more interesting things occupying her mind than notions of her own beauty.

When they reached the wide field that separated the two ranches, Elmira's and her neighbour's, the three cows lifted their heads at the sound of the bucket as if knowing what was to come. They stood in close proximity to each other. They stepped back, kicking their hind legs out, mooing loudly. The deep sound reverberated around them. Houdini was fascinated by their patchy black and white coats, their flaring nostrils, the bulk of them, and their heavy udders. Intrigued by the flickers in their sad eyes, he observed carefully, as if they, too, had fragmented daydreams inside them. Elmira clicked her tongue, approached the middle cow, and gently stroked its body, whispering Portuguese. After placing the bucket under its udders, she waved Houdini closer. He held a teat, tugging firmly. He tugged until blood spurted out, hitting the bucket at a diagonal angle. He tugged again: more blood. The cow groaned, wide-eyed and heavy with the burden of a vision that had taken root inside it.

Later, Houdini removed four stillborns who had found their way to the pigsty, crawling gleefully in the dirt. Two tried to slip through the gaps of the gate in the fence. He removed another two from Elmira's pantry, their mouths purple with beetroot. He temporarily fixed the gate, tying it closed with a long cable wire that had split. It offered its multi-coloured veins to those who crossed the entrance. He tried to think of a solution for the cows leaking blood, seeing fragments of the visions inside them splintering off into different afternoons.

By the end of that day, Elmira sat him down at the worn wooden kitchen table. The babies crawled between them. The kettle whistled on the stove.

'Tell me about the other boys in Batch Two,' she said, clasping his shoulder with one hand, holding a bottle of pesticide in the other.

By their third week together, another vision of marauding gargoyles was loose on the ranch. Elmira had sketched it three days before, knowing its corners, and spilled her beads there. The gargoyles tore through the ranch leaving things in disarray. Houdini spent half a day fixing it all during an aftermath of silence.

They settled into a routine over the next few months. Every two weeks, the stillborns had to be recharged, their wires connected to battery packs Elmira stored in the barn. Houdini helped Elmira sell her vegetables at the farmer's market on the weekends. He cleaned out the barn after the chaos of the babies, checked the cows, fed the alpacas, looked after the four horses, helped tidy the main house. He fed the one pig Elmira wouldn't kill. It refused to sleep in the sty and could often be found lying on the kitchen floor snorting into the night. If you tried to catch it, it deftly shot through the open kitchen door, pink, wily, in search of another patch to claim for the evening.

Sometimes Houdini waved away the coyotes that circled the ranch in hopes of finding food or waste. They were bright-eyed and knowing. Their cries ebbed away in the dark, companions to distant ancestors. Elmira was often holed up in her room at night, sketching or sewing oversized clothes for the babies, for visions she dared not name. In his memory bank, Houdini filed away the image of her body caving into tiredness, the sewing-machine slyly attempting to sew her mouth while she slept, a cow's foot on the pedal leaking blood.

One night, Houdini sat on the steps outside the kitchen, the waft of blackberry pie still in the air, heat from the oven warm on his skin, the sky vast and unknowable, the stillborns mumbling at their wires that doubled as umbilical cords. He was thinking of the boys in Batch 2, wondering about their roles as sons, firing stones from his catapult into the night, when he spotted a figure in the distance. A man. His gait was confident, purposeful. He carried something in each hand: a kill.

A crack of silver shot across the sky, then another, rattling

to cause uneven constellations, shaking the ranch's founda-
tions. More cracks roared above. The cows headed for the
barn. The horses fled to one outhouse. The pig shrieked.
The alpacas ran to a second outhouse. Then the man was
rushing from the claws of the night, passing the pigsty, the
barn, the outhouses, onto the snaky path towards Houdini,
whose catapult ceased coughing stones.

The coyote heads slipped through the catapult instead.
This was how Calhoun burst into their lives, like Noah into
Elmira's ark. Chuckling when he should have been scared,
carrying two dead armadillos, a bag strapped to his back,
spilling lightning from his mouth.

Elmira rushed down the hallway into the kitchen, holding
a pair of scissors in one hand, a trail of checked red cloth
in the other.

'What the hell is going on?' she asked, irritated at being
disturbed, annoyed by the sight of a stranger in her kitchen.

'Wowee! It's lethal out there. I'm Calhoun, Cal for short.
Just looking for a bed to call my own for one evening.' He
laughed, like a man who'd just come off a rollercoaster ride
rather than escaping the possibility of being struck dead by
lightning.

Houdini loitered by the humming freezer, adding, 'He
brought armadillos.'

'I can see that!' Elmira responded, still a little annoyed.

'Are you going to use those on me?' Cal asked, watching

Elmira's slightly shaky hands, the thick Afro curls, the rhythm of her chest rising and falling, the hint of wildness in her eyes.

Elmira set the scissors on the wooden countertop. 'Give him a root beer.' She glanced at the armadillos on her table, dead-eyed yet staring at the light. A film of dust fell at an angle, like a sprinkling of dirty stardust.

Houdini opened the freezer. Misty cold air spilled out in relief. He handed the bottle to Cal, who peeled off the lid with his teeth before taking a long, slow, satisfied swig. Cal was rumpled, craggily handsome, dark-haired and dark-eyed. Not quite skinny but not quite stocky either: a man of in-betweens. Elmira spotted the crescent-shaped red scars on the backs of his hands, like angry half-thoughts never fully formed.

Noticing her expression, Cal placed the bottle on the table and stepped back. 'They're from the chemical plant, the one behind the old shipping yard.'

'I thought they closed that place,' Elmira said, shooing him towards the table as though directing one of her cows.

He smiled at her lacklustre hostess skills. 'Well, they open it now and again. A few of us got called back for work there. It's closed for several cycles so I thought I'd follow the wind for a bit.'

'The wind is temperamental,' Elmira said, setting the long piece of cloth down, fishing a pair of red oven gloves from one of the drawers.

'I wouldn't have her any other way.' Cal rested his grey duffel bag against the table. His khaki shirt bore stains at the armpits. He grabbed the root beer and took a seat, settling back into the chair. He stretched out his legs, watching Elmira fuss at the stove as if he'd always done so.

'I'll help you fix the gate properly,' he added, a man used to bargaining when necessary.

Houdini, catapult in hand, took a seat, too, at the head of the table. He pulled the catapult string back, smiling mechanically at Cal at the opposite end.

'I suppose you might want some blackberry pie with your root beer?' Elmira offered, spinning around, hands in gloves.

'I suppose I might.' Cal kneaded his neck. Then he flicked the root-beer lid he'd kept in his pocket right through the catapult, startling Houdini.

Houdini dropped the catapult against his thigh. He noticed the stillborns hadn't come out to greet Cal the way they had with him. He smiled at the thought.

The atmosphere was charged, although he couldn't identify why. It was like the day Elmira met him at the bridge. Only different. The night was full of possibilities: the armadillos might rise from the table to chase the chaos of lightning, the long trail of checked cloth fluttering between them all in a game of cloth, scissors, catapult, man.

*

Of course Cal stayed longer than one night. Damage from the lightning had lifted the main gate completely, tossing it several metres away. A meteorite-shaped hole was left in the barn roof. The doors of two outhouses had cracks in them, as if unencumbered bolts had rattled through in search of items to destroy. The morning after, Cal surveyed the damage calmly, a cigarette smoking from the corner of his mouth. 'It could have been worse, young blood,' he commented.

Houdini was forced to trail him, since he and Elmira didn't know this stranger well enough. He stood by his side on the snaky path looking out into the distance. They listened to the sounds in the area colliding: a crow in panicked flight, horses galloping from another ranch. Gargoyles that had slept in the lines of the land emerged, with hearts floating in the darkness of their chests. Houdini sensed the arrival of a man who could outrun lightning bolts had somehow dented his and Elmira's existence at the ranch. He surveyed the scars on the back of Cal's hands discreetly, as if they'd have answers, somehow willingly betray him.

'The babies don't seem to like you,' Houdini said, as they walked down the path, a small note of triumph in his tone. Their footsteps crunched along the stones, top dog, underdog.

Cal took a long drag from the cigarette before answering. 'Have you ever seen a pig in a wedding dress, young blood? A person might one day, if they drink enough of whatever makes them high. Just don't ask them what it is they're drinking or how the pig got into the dress.'

Cal fixed the gate and the barn's roof, filled the cracks in the outhouse doors. He built Elmira a storage unit for her sewing materials from leftover wood. Her bright cloths spilled like coloured, irrational waterfalls from the shelves. He cooked them armadillo in a dark plum sauce. At dinner, he revealed he was the son of a Chippewa wanderer; tracking was in his blood. He told them contradictions in people shouldn't be curbed, that he liked them in his meals on occasion. Houdini watched Elmira's half-smile linger, her eyes on those scarred hands that seemed useful for many things.

Cal took him whitetail hunting, surrounded by hundreds of breathing trees, their weathered barks silently communicating with the icy air. The cry of the odd hawk was a welcome interruption in large acres of woodland. In the distance, the lake glimmered. Reflections from its cold, watery eye fell on hard-trodden patches of ground, clusters of crackling leaves. Cal and Houdini hunkered down behind a tree, watching the deer ahead darting to and fro, pausing now and again to lower its head to the ground.

Cal blew breath on his fingers, curled and uncurled them in preparation. 'Keep still for now, young blood,' he said, voice a whisper. He removed the Remington shotgun from his back. 'Don't alarm the fella.'

Houdini stuffed a hand into his pocket, rubbing his broken catapult strap. Elmira hadn't checked on him this morning the way she had done on the bridge that first day. In fact, she hadn't checked him first thing for a few days. She seemed distracted, holed up in her room, feverishly drawing the visions she'd birthed. He assessed the gun's length, its efficiency, its deadly nozzle: a weapon capturing the breathing of creatures scurrying in the background. As the deer reappeared in their line of vision, Cal raised the gun, aimed, fired.

The shot rang out. The deer stumbled in a short, drunken ceremony of death.

'Ha-ha! Come on.' Cal sprang up quickly. They ran to the deer. It lay on its side, bleeding from the neck, the light in its eyes waning.

'Don't fight it, boy,' Cal said. 'You'll live again in some other way.' His tone was almost empathetic. 'Come on, help me with it.'

Houdini stretched out his arms. A hypnotised expression appeared on his face. He couldn't help lift the deer. Instead his arms moved back and forth, trapped in the same mechanical motion. He saw Elmira's head on the deer's body, spilling blue beads from her mouth.

When they arrived back at the ranch, the babies crawled out to greet them, circling their feet excitedly. Cal ignored them the way he always did. The deer's mouth was sealed shut with Cal's red scars from the chemical plant.

*

That night, watching them from the crack of her bedroom door left slightly open, Houdini found Cal and Elmira in bed. Their bodies were entangled, slick. Cal was breathing against her breasts, his hands on her rippling back. Houdini walked to his own room, crawled into bed unsteadily. Looking up at the white ceiling, he saw their bodies again. This time covered with plum sauce. The elements of images filed away had collided again. The plum sauce attempted to outrun Elmira's bright cloths, broken free from their cubicles. Elmira and Cal were not far behind, naked, hunting for the things they'd created. The last image he saw before closing his eyes was of Elmira pinned high up on the outside wall of the barn, almost touching the roof. There was a large, cavernous hole in her stomach, opening and closing sporadically. He and Cal climbed up the wall, he holding his broken catapult, Cal with his shotgun strapped to his back. When they reached Elmira, they took turns dipping their weapons into the cavernous hole. The sound of her sewing-machine stuttered in the background, trying to sew without any material. They crawled into her stomach, transported to a night beyond it. Arriving to find they'd lost their weapons, the sky was raining milk. And the babies had grown to boys with wires as umbilical cords dangling from their backs. Houdini's final thought was that Elmira didn't need him any more.

*

By the fifth month, Elmira was convinced Houdini had been displaying signs of anger. But how could that be possible? Yet she was certain. He hadn't helped her sell vegetables for weeks or do the errands in town she relied on him for. And she had been feeding the homeless who circled the ranch by herself, a task they'd done together. Lately, she saw why he called them coyotes as they pressed hungry wolf-like faces through the gaps of the fence, rattling the gates, darkened arms encrusted with dirt, hands outstretched, gaunt and hollowed. Once, she discovered one hiding in an outhouse, a gas mask on his face, Houdini using his catapult to fire stones at him, a gargoyle wrestling the mask off.

It was a warm June afternoon when she checked Houdini's room to find it empty. Her sketches of Noah's Ark had crosses on the animals' faces, holes cut out of their bodies. In her pantry, the beetroots were smashed, strewn all over the floor. Ill-fitting adult clothes for her visions, for her babies to play with, had been burned. Like mocking singed silhouettes thrown on the roof, the fence, in the pigsty.

He had malfunctioned.

She was sure of it. There was nobody to tell. Cal had disappeared two days before. Gone in the night because that was what drifters did, his blood mutated from working in a chemical plant. They held your nipples with scarred hands, fired a shotgun at their dreams to leave a glinting piece contorting in your chest, cooked lovingly to sell you an illusion. They built you things to soften the blow so that, one day, they would leave.

Elmira found the cabinet Cal had crafted on the stairs, chipped and collapsed in parts. Her materials were gone. Her sewing instruments were left in the sink, silvery and inadequate in the unforgiving light of day.

Outside, the gas masks were left on the path, ominous in the glare of light, as though they'd been secretly trying to breathe. Gargoyles took turns to put them on. Her bright materials were scattered around the undulating field, taunting the confused cows, whose udders had ruptured. They groaned in agony while the rainbow cloths twisted, shifted and trembled, like sly intermissions. Elmira raised her arms to comfort the cows. Tears ran down her cheeks. A spotted purple cloth fluttered to a cow's face, blurring it momentarily, rendering it irrelevant. She realised in her panic she had missed something. She ran to the barn again. Shoved the door open with all her strength. They were gone.

She found all nine drones tied to the gate destroyed, wires ripped out, retractable heads smashed in. She screamed. Her babies, her drones, which measured the health of her produce and made her feel safe on the ranch, were defunct. Frantically she untied them, watching each one drop to the ground. The sound of the gate swinging to offload their weight reverberated. The drones shrivelled up into thirsty, misshapen visions. The pain in her head was so bad, Elmira worried it would crack in two, a garish gift for the afternoon. She reached for their wires wilting in the hot air. A note from Houdini was pinned to the gate that read:

Gone in search of the yolk from my daydreams.

Houdini had been walking for exactly twenty minutes when he reached the school. A few memories flooded in: returning two cans of violet paint to Ed at the hardware store because Elmira had seen the bodies of homeless people fading in a purple room, holding rusted medical instruments, the bi-monthly horticultural meeting at the former gasworks, the pop-up saloon they'd built for the spring fair with other members of the town's steering committee, Elmira laughing and serving drinks from the saloon to groups of people gathered around. Houdini detonated then. The blast from his body wrecked the school, the church, the gas station, killing the coyotes living as street kings, shattering surrounding factories and houses.

There was nothing left of him, as intended.

In the small, forgotten towns of Midwestern America, mirrorings of this occurred as the other five boys from Batch 2 detonated. Just before, a series of identification numbers inside them flashed: X2467A, NZT452, K4734, Y67429, P124XKW. Then the word *ESCALATE* glowing amber.

Their mothers for this cycle were left bereft. They stood on bridges or underpasses, in the doorways of abandoned buildings and ranches, howling about blue-eyed robot bombs that doubled as their children. They undressed, frightened by what the next rotation of children would bring, willing to be impregnated by the damaged gargoyles of the land instead.

Nudibranch

Nudibranch: soft-bodied, marine gastropod molluscs, which shed their shells after their larval stage. They are noted for their often extraordinary colours and striking forms.

When the goddess Kiru emerges from the shoreline on the small island of St Simeran, the third hand in her stomach lining contracts, steering her towards the sounds of the eunuchs surrounding a large fire on the beach, shrouded in an orange glow from the flames. The eunuchs are hollering, mating calls that are like war-cries. Privates exposed, they stand in a loose circle rushing back towards the fire, beating their chests while the carrier pigeons fluttering above shed feathers on their bare skin. Kiru waits patiently on the sidelines. Her third hand drops soft-bodied, lightning-coloured seeds in the space between their heartbeats. It is Haribas, the festival of love for eunuchs. Every five years, eunuchs gather to celebrate, maybe find someone special, slits from their lost or dysfunctional penises tumbling in the dark corners of the heavens. Kiru steadies her breathing, watching. Salt water in her mouth leaves a tangy taste. Pressed against the night, she has already changed its shape into a mountain face that travels when white water lapping its lines evaporates. Fragmented moonlight gives proceedings an ethereal appearance. Mist curls and uncurls to reveal things seductively, slowly. Squashed Guinness cans sink into the sand. A gentle breeze passing through makes them hollow, unexpected instruments punctuating the main event. There are jagged mountains in the distance with handfuls of uranium inside, rumbling quietly. A bloodstained scroll is planted in the sand before Kiru at an angle. Huts dotted around the island on stilts have orbs of orange light piercing through tiny holes. Slick, moist fossils languish amid stones, in moss-carpeted pockets, on cool rocks that anchor the flailing hands of a dawn. The eunuchs have clouds in their mouths; their motions are erratic, as though they'll fall into the fire one by one backwards. They soften each other's injuries with white puffs of breath. They are burning the clothes they arrived in. The sound of fire races to meet bright molluscs in a space that expands and shrinks as things unfold. The carrier pigeons squawk, producing a din that sounds like black rain falling at an angle on the heads of stillborns, like a crow beak tapping against the entrance of Kiru's cold womb, like the screeching from going blind temporarily travelling through a tortoise shell in the sky, then falling into the water with shell markings that cause flurries, breaches and an undulating silence. They mimic the sound of a lung sinking, chasing an echo thinking it can catch it.

The mating cries of the eunuchs rise, travelling across the island to soft-bodied women emerging through the soil, the whites in their eye sockets morphing into irises of every hue. Mist bleeds red at the edges, seeping into a rough-hewn mountain that will use a sarong as a bandage over its mouth at some point.

The warm-bodied women uproot from all corners of the island bearing drunken tongues from wine spilled in the island's earth for seven days before proceedings. They rush towards the mating cries, nipples puckered, mouths pliable, momentarily curbed by night dew. They are of the earth. Kiru has an advantage, being of the water. She bends down to lick blood off the scroll, blows her breath inside it to see how the cream-coloured paper will interpret it. Small orange blobs shaped like tiny micro-organisms shimmer on the scroll. She smiles; she has come to fall in love.

> *For now Kiru*
> *Is a woman*
> *From Algeria*
> *With dark hair*

swishing down her back and an easy, charming smile. She is wearing a black bikini. The blue shift over it is damp at the bottom, occasionally clinging to her thighs, bearing small trails of sand.

After the burning ceremony, she picks up Matthew, a scientist from a makeshift bar on the beach; light off the huts casts a warm glow on their skin. The soft-bodied women pair off with men who are still high from their ritual. There is alcohol flowing, a social lubricant that makes any gathering less awkward. Kiru assesses these women clinically, knowing their flaws will rise to the surface of clear water before breaking through. She listens for it. Matthew is talkative, eager. They laugh, carrying their drinks to the back end of the beach, deep into the belly of trees and land that feels joyously remote. There is the occasional rare white orchid, and empty alcohol bottles contain formations of past nights. Music from a stage at the far end of the beach filters through. Gulping rum, they are joined by iguanas eating sap from the pale trees that makes them dazed, and one-eyed water crickets from a tale man forgot to include in the Bible.

I'm so happy I burned the clothes I arrived in! Matthew flicks a petal from his Hawaiian patterned shorts. Oh, yes! It's liberating, as if a shackle's been broken. There is something in the air here. I feel like another version of myself. And the women fuck!

We can do anything here.

You are like Einstein, Kiru offers, pulling him closer. Like his equation of general relativity, mutating in the fabric of space and time.

Yes! he says, a look of wonder in his eyes at her, the surroundings, the possibilities.

I am $Gpv = 8\pi G$ $(Tuv + p\ n\ g\ v\ v)$.

He knocks back his drink. Matthew considers himself a eunuch because of his impotency. She tells him about the shape and girth of an invisible penis he will gain by the time the night is over.

Do you know what betrayal tastes like? she asks.

There is a burden to carrying salty alphabets on my tongue.

Matthew blinks up at her, heady, tipsy, a little confused.

Three hours pass. Kiru becomes annoyed. She cannot imagine Matthew reaching for the sound of bones tumbling in water, succumbing to being realigned in the frothing white, stark against it, brightly lit, and carrying mouthfuls of seaweed with stories of their own to tell. She realises she cannot love him. His receding hairline elicits sympathy, not attraction. His snaggle-toothed breathy revelations about science had begun to grate. He would yammer on endlessly until she strangled him on the shoreline.

Catching him unaware, she sticks her fingers into his chest, melting flesh. The charred scent rising up to their nostrils as a pattern of smoke unwinds from his chest, shaped like small nudibranch. She reaches through bone, a blueprint at birth washed away by the pumping of blood. Her fingers reach further in, finding his misshapen heart. She runs a finger over the muscle, over the pumping rhythm she has already caught with the damp folds of her vagina. He is hypnotised by the gleam in her eyes, the baring of her teeth, the lightning-blue lines of light running beneath her skin as though she is a circuit.

Her fingers grab his heart, pulling it right out. A sucking sound ensues, followed by a vacuum.

He makes an aaargh noise. It is surprise. It is relief. It is tender.

A carrier pigeon hovers above, shedding a feather that tumbles into the vacuum in his chest, skimming the last conversation he had with an air stewardess once on an easy-Jet flight about the weight of atoms. The feather tumbling in the dark will change colour once it hits the bottom. The carrier pigeon will report this to others in its flock.

Kiru finds a quiet spot to eat his heart, beneath a tree oozing sap, enjoying the shelter under its drooping white palm-like leaves. She is ravenous. His heart tastes of cigarettes, red wine, tiny bits of aluminium, of small murmurs machines hadn't detected yet. She polishes it off in four bites, licking her fingers clean. Then, she stands beneath the ghostly tree holding her arms up to the light; she sheds her skin.

Now she is
Afro-haired
Long-limbed
And brown-skinned

with the pretty face of a young woman in Cuba who runs a stall making small art pieces from food, who has a beauty mark on her face that changes position slightly depending on the humidity.

She finds Patrice smashing a lobster's head on a rock. He has an elaborate, cartoon-like moustache, which tickles her funny bone, and a Romanian accent.

Are you enjoying the festival? Kiru asks.

Oh, yes! Very much. It's nice to be around other men like me.

You mean other eunuchs?

Well ... you know, men who understand. I've been celibate for five years. Now I want to break that vow.

I am understanding. I understand that people who die through sudden accidents don't know they're lucky because it's quick. I understand when you destroy something you give it the opportunity to be born again.

I'll take your word for it! What an unusual creature you are. He is drawn by the smoothness of her skin, the beauty spot he cannot take his eyes off for some reason.

I can re-enact one of your strongest memories. Would you like to see?

Surely there's only one answer to that! He is smiling. His mind is distracted by the lobster dangling from his fingers, dripping rivulets of water onto his feet. Badly injured, the lobster is attempting to escape to the second shoreline the carrier pigeons have drawn with their beaks.

Kiru re-enacts his most indelible teenage memory: when he rescues a boy from a house fire. It was terrifying, exciting. He was driven by instinct, recklessness, adrenalin. He watches open-mouthed, astounded that she knows this. Her blue shift rides up her thighs a little as she performs.

Later, she discovers that Patrice's wife died five years before. Of course he is saddened by his loss. She is sad about this unfortunate turn of events.

She cannot compete with his dead wife or the memories she left behind that float and duck between his organs. She wants to leave a bite mark on his collarbone that he will stroke even after they've faded. She wants to breathe against the pulse in his neck as though she can tame its movements with her breaths.

I'll build a new penis for you from a current, she says. Not leave you with the old one that still carries the touch of your wife's fingertips.

He laughs uncomfortably, replying, When I was a teenager I used to dream of Pam Grier sitting on the edge of my bed holding a rocket.

She smiles at this. It is a sincere curving of her plump

lips, which are intoxicating to him. Kiru wants to apologise for the things she cannot tell him.

If only you could hit your head on rocks below shimmering surfaces of water and not be fazed by the impact or your blood momentarily blinding fish.

If only you were how I imagined you to be.

What do I do with the disappointment of this? With the gap in between?

What do I store there for cold, isolating winters you will not be a part of?

She eats half of Patrice's heart in the early hours of the morning when the island is still asleep. She dumps the other half in the waters of the blue sea for a whale that has recently given birth in the Pacific, longing for the call of its young. She recalls the gathering of carrier pigeons swallowing patterns of nudibranch-shaped smoke from Patrice's chest, the shed feather turning to gold in the darkened vacuum of his chest.

Small golden triangles rise to the surface of Kiru's skin. She glows in the hazy grey light of dawn, watching mist softening the lines of mountains for what the day will bring. The island's creatures create a gentle din to run her fingers over.

A tear runs down Kiru's cheek. She is lonely. She wants to fill the ache that grows inside her, that isn't knowable no matter which corner of herself she reaches it from, no matter whose footsteps she temporarily borrows to do so. It is vast. And she is like a small chess queen loose in the sky, clutching at shapes, at possibilities that amount to nothing as she opens her hand on the crash down.

After she sheds her skin, she watches it in the water. It is like a diving suit with a face, carried away by ripples.

She does not know what it is like to have female friends. She spends two to three hours interacting with the soft-bodied women who speak as if words are foreign objects in their mouths, whose lungs she can hear shrinking while the iguanas crawl around the island without heads that have vanished.

Late in the afternoon Kiru rests in one of several boats moored on the island. She thinks of the stray items the soft-bodied women have begun to stash away: two fire extinguishers, a telescope, a high wooden chair with a dirty velvet seat, three propellers, and two cable cars. She panics with her eyes closed, as she is prone to doing occasionally. She is tired from the energy she expends prowling the island. Her tiredness results in strange visions that carve a path through the day. She dreams of a catastrophic dark-ness where everything falls away one by one, orbiting in a black star-studded distance above the earth with warped frequencies that result in it all falling down again in the wrong place: with the sea now a glimmering sky, the sky a weightless, cloud-filled ground, rock faces hiding in caves, mountains made of the island's creatures leaking tree sap, trees uprooted in panicked flight, alcohol bottles filled with new weather shot through with spots of ice, eunuchs emerging from a fire charred, offering to hide bits of their lives in shed skin. When light from the black star-studded space above the earth threatens to split her head in two, Kiru sees herself sitting on top of the mountain of island creatures eating fossils one by one but she knows this will not do. She clambers out of the boat.

By the time she finds Ray from Madagascar fixing one leg of the stage at the far end of the beach, Kiru is

A curvy Mediterranean
Beauty with a
Boyishly short
Pixie cut.

Amber nudibranch from the telescope lens have made their way to them but Ray has not spotted this. He is wiry, handsome, a little sweaty from his efforts. He has a brutish slash of a mouth. As if things had accidents there. Other men pass to wander the island's pathways, mountains and peaks. Some emerge from the beach huts with daylight waning in their eyes. By now the soft-bodied women, her competitors, are gasping for air between conversations, grabbing bits of sand that slide through their fingers.

Can I help you? Kiru tugs down her shift, watching Ray's head.

No, thanks. Don't move, though, he instructs. Somehow you standing there is making this task more bearable.

Why are you fixing the stage?

He chuckles, throws her a bemused look. Because if I don't some musicians among us might get injured.

You cannot fix all the world's stages. What do they do when you are not there to help? Injury is part of living.

This is true but I can't just leave it knowing people could get hurt. Besides, I have a soft spot for musicians. I think I may have been one in a past life.

What are you in this life? She kneels then, sinking into the sand, shallow pockets to catch odd bits of conversation.

The stage is even again. He dusts his hands on his backside. I'm a fisherman.

Something in her turns cold. A thin film of frost finds its way into her insides.

She sees herself dangling from a hook in the ceiling of his shop, bright purple. He is surprised that she has adjusted to the air of the shop despite the hook inside her trying to catch things that take on different forms. Despite the hunger she will spread to other creatures, who do not know what it means to truly be insatiable, dissatisfied. She knows to listen to her visions when they come. Her eyes are patient, understanding. He feels compelled to say, I don't know what instrument I played in a past life.

I can tell you, she says. She stands. Tiny spots of blood on her shift have dried to a barely noticeable decoration. She begins to make the noise of an instrument that feels familiar, that sounds eerily accurate, like a horn maybe, yet he cannot place it.

They hang around the stage area into the evening, watching a series of performances and fireworks exploding in the sky that she imagines assembling into bright lava-filled tongues. Later, they go for a walk.

Tell me how you became a eunuch, she encourages, touching his arm.

Overhead, the carrier pigeons drop blank scrolls in different parts of the island.

I had testicular cancer.

I'm sorry for your cancer.

Don't be, he says. We killed it.

They hold hands. Intermittently, he tries to guess which instrument she mimicked.

He is unsuccessful.

On her walk back through the trees, the gauzy light, and beneath the knowing bold sky, Kiru eats Ray's heart naked, mouth smudged red. How could she place her heart, her future in the hands of a man who didn't even know what instrument he was destined to play? His heart tastes like a small night tucked in the plain sight of a morning, like standing on a brink with your arms outstretched, like eating a new kind of fruit that bleeds. She notices the soft-bodied women are now in the white trees, shrieking.

Over the next four days of Haribas, Kiru eats seven more hearts. By the time she heads back to the shoreline on the last day to sleep in white waters, she is now

> *A little girl*
> *Sporting pigtails, pregnant*
> *From eating the hearts*
> *Of ten men.*

She hopes to fall in love one day. For now, she hollers, a call that signifies the end of a mating season for her. A hallowed echo the mountains and mist recognise but sends panic into the crevices of an island rupturing; clusters of uranium erupt, rooftops of huts catch fire; life rafts made from felled trees dot the shoreline, waiting for something dark and sly to hatch on them; moored boats hold the soft-bodied women from the earth, only able to breathe for four days before running out of their allocated air. But the eunuchs are not dead. They are trapped on the island, dazed, meandering around without hearts wondering why the musical instruments buck in the water, why the carrier pigeons are now one-winged and blind, circling scrolls with guidance for the next festival. Kiru leaves St Simeran in this state.

It is
An alchemy
A purging
A morning sitting on
Its backside
A thing of wonder fluttering
In the periphery of
A god's vision.

Daishuku

There'd been four occurrences of his body bending time backwards. Nobody would believe it but it had. Here. In this instance, he was fifty, fallen through the speckled void into London, languishing in one strip of intersecting subways pulsing like the city's varicose veins. Here. Elephant and Castle. Night time. Homeless. A howl in competition with the roundabout's traffic lights, the screeching of tyres, impatient bodies milling about. Daishuku prised his cold lids open as if to counter the ache in numbed fingers clutching a Styrofoam cup of tea he didn't remember, of course he didn't. He'd inherited the tea, the frost, the oil spillage on the steps leading in, the smell of chips in hastily coned paper, the patter of footsteps streaming to and fro, the looks of contempt, the swirl of coats hiding invisible pregnancies in thin linings, the occasional drop of coins threatening to scatter the murmurings of his head, like mosquito legs in the cold. He took a sip of the tea, shoulder-length stringy hair streaked with grey dipping forward. Mouth warmed, he gulped some more, a dark trail running into his beard. He set the cup down with a shaky hand, his knuckles red, the skin around it pale and thin, a cluster of tiny brown spots edging towards his fingers. He patted himself down slowly. He was clothed in rags; the scent of sweat mixed with beer lingered. He tasted beer in his throat, beneath the bland warmth of tea. Worn plimsolls on his feet were wrapped in white plastic bags. He considered the sum of his new beginning. Its parts separated in the dank subway. He considered the bleakness of it, crawling gently towards stained chip paper refashioned into greasy blueprints. He began to chant, 'Daishuku.' A name. A memory on his tongue. He poked coins in the silver bowl before him. A fleeting image appeared: the grotesque shopping mall's pink elephant drinking oil from the subway steps before skidding on the ice, breaking its neck to interrupt the overwhelming feeling of loneliness.

After a few hours, the influx of commuters waned to occasional figures dribbling in different directions, bearing cracked mouths from mopping spillage at the edges. Daishuku inhaled deeply, a weightless passage of air twisting within him, uprooting organs. He pictured those organs growing on trees, as fruit lining the pavements, lungs weighing down branches, kidneys protruding from the base, heart growing out of the trunk: a decorative gift, a bloody, plump, garish Christmas bauble, a world in disguise. The underpass swam. He felt light-headed. He was used to this. *Why are you always ungrateful for your inher-itance?* he asked himself silently. *Not through what you say but by your body's reactions.*

He tipped the silver bowl, stashed the coins in his trouser pockets. Above, the voices of teenagers gleefully arguing filtered through. He flexed his fingers, placed his hands on the bowl. He raised his head up, opened his mouth. The tear on the inside of his left cheek happened in split seconds. He ran the tip of his tongue over it, giving it a permission of sorts. It oozed a multi-coloured concoction that flooded his mouth, lined his tongue like an ambrosia. He spat into the bowl. A quiet conduit that could upend the items from wreckages, pin them into a labyrinth of doorways in the dark. He rummaged inside his black jacket, which had the word *Awake* printed on the back in blue let-tering. He pulled out a scruffy white handkerchief with a spider's diagram of the surrounding area, the words *Station, London College of Communications, Bus Stop, Shopping Mall and Pink Elephant* circled. He stood up awkwardly, leaned against the wall listening, gathering himself. He pushed off into his stride, like a swimmer into a stroke. These were his alarm bells, indications the timer had started: an injury producing a small rainbow, a rumbling from an internal opening, which meant he needed to move. The bright-coloured mucus in the bowl shimmered, thinning, liquefying. Daishuku headed into the night, coins jangling in his pockets becoming moonshine against his fingers, the heads and tails of fortune wrestling on zebra crossings while traffic lights sang.

He shuffled along in the cold, noting the swirl of night activity with the eye of an outsider: handfuls of people at each bus stop spilling in and out of large red buses pulling to a stop by seated shelters, the glow from the one remaining stall shuddering, the man inside selling confectionery, lighters, cigarette cases, blowing on his hands intermittently. The odd lampposts springing from pavements were tall, steadfast, unacknowledged guardians of the city. He coughed on the handkerchief; tiny bright spots appeared over the diagram. He shoved it back into his pocket. The plastic bags on his feet kept getting caught along the pavement so he untied them, dumping them in an overflowing bin. A rush of frosty air crept through the holes in his plimsolls, a wind through his soles. He walked to the pink elephant, placed the handkerchief beneath it, moonshine on top. He knew in the wake of his departure, when the timer stopped between the slowly eroding bodies on concrete pathways, some would become smudged in the fog, unaware when men like him borrowed their costumes, leaving fingerprints fading along the edges of their lives, building waning refuges on cold shoulders that could be toppled by a breath. He felt small in the fortress of the city, a broken atom in a big tattered coat, the big coat flying above roaring, a robust, darkened cloud jacket spilling corn grains from its pockets, below, at the roundabout, the car tyres skidding on grains, on soft points of earth that had travelled through pockets. A raucous group of men from a stag do passed him; one spilled beer on him, patting him on the back, handing him a Monopoly note. His friends laughed.

Another harassed-looking man wielding a briefcase spat, barely missing him. A woman pushing a pram filled with shopping but no baby forced him into the road. The ache in his chest deepened. This was what it was like to lose everything. He knew this feeling. It never stopped hurting. He spotted a baguette in a Sainsbury's bag poking from another bin. He picked up the pace, noting people didn't acknowledge him except to express their silent disdain, their superiority, their relief that these weren't their circumstances.

They weren't responsible for any of it.

He spoke broken Japanese mixed with English to the tube-station attendant, who wore what looked like a large orange bib over his uniform. *Have you seen my Mae?* He asked. *Mae keep Alzheimer's in suitcase.* Daishuku shifted his weight from one foot to the other. The attendant pressed a button on his walkie-talkie. A static sound emanated briefly, like a television channel that hadn't been tuned in. He motioned to the opposite side, pinched features more pronounced as he spoke. *Follow that road round, then all the way down, about twenty minutes' walk. There's a shelter and soup kitchen. You want to get there as soon as possible. It gets pretty full up by now but they will HELP you, okay, hmm?*

Daishuku pointed in the same direction repeatedly. *I go down, go down!* he announced, as if it were a revelation. The attendant nodded patiently, smiling stiffly, already turning away to indicate the conversation was over. Daishuku left the station entrance, his feet frozen, plimsolls damp from light rain. He pressed his hand against his rib as a sharp pain shot through it, the collapse of a small bone growing in the wrong direction. He heard the shattering in his peripheral vision, like autumn from a black smoked bottle. He saw small nails falling from the sky. Though attuned to these occurrences, these unexplained growths on the margins, they left him disoriented. Bright spots from his mouth were now on his coat, becoming patches. The patches became claws; the claws changed to bright, blind gulls. The blind gulls lost their heads to the city's rooftops bejewelled with raindrops, left their bodies to hatch memories in subways and underpasses, their feathers runny in bowls exposed to the elements, the distant chime of coins serenading the bowls' rims, the nails from the sky piercing their heartbeats. Their margins were thumbed, lifted edges where they were runny claws in ribs, while Daishuku's bone breathed in a damp plimsoll.

The periphery loomed. Wet tendrils of hair stuck to his neck. He hurried on. He followed the station attendant's instructions, pressing the bell of the red-brick building with the sign *St Michael's Shelter and Kitchen*. Had the station man really meant go dawn? Stay till dawn. *Yes! Go dawn.*

A curly-haired, rail-thin young woman answered, earnest and warm. She wore a striped apron over her navy T-shirt and jeans, a roll of tinfoil in one hand. She ushered him into a small reception area with certificates and photographs on the walls, briefly addressing a heavily tattooed, pink-haired lady at the front desk, who was slotting sheets of paper onto a clipboard. The desk was filled with leaflets; an open jar of peanuts sat at the edge. On one wall, a full notice-board contained a staff family tree. Beneath that stood a grey radiator making a *Suump!* sucking sound as though a magnet kept trying to land inside it. *You find Mae?* Daishuku asked, addressing the thin woman. *Mae come here?* He searched the woman's features. She tucked the tinfoil beneath her arm, a furrow appearing on her brow. *I'm afraid we haven't had a Mae here this evening. You're welcome to stay the night, though.* Gently, she drew him into the large hall. It smelt of soups, bread, warm spices, like somebody's kitchen, a hearth burning slowly in the guts of a red home for vagrants. There were bodies everywhere; a musty scent lingered in the air. At one end, lines of people queuing for food, slack badminton nets piled behind a row of volunteers serving from pots and pans. At the other end lay bodies in sleeping bags, blankets over them, breathing to mechanise the hearth. After eating a bowl of mildly flavoured chicken soup, Daishuku scanned his surroundings, watching for Mae to appear in the gaps between figures, at the end of the clinking of cutlery. He saw her face unfolding from the roll of tinfoil, crinkled, Mae as a tiny tattoo running up the reception-ist's arm, in the jar of peanuts trying to break through holding a soiled blueprint, inside the radiator attempting to embrace an elusive magnet. He tried to hold all these sightings of his Mae but couldn't. It was red mist slipping through his fingers, faint trails that amounted to noth-ing, limping around the hearth. He fell asleep, between memories in the wrong order, a blanket over him, barely reaching his feet.

Later, the pain in his chest woke him up. And somebody had stolen his shoes, inheriting the wind in his soles, a shrill whistling at the opposite end reclaiming it as an ancestor. The pain he felt rocketing through his body was unbearable, searing. His nerves hummed as though a thousand knives were pinned against them. The ache in his head threatened to split it, like an unsweetened coconut. He convulsed, curled into a ball amid other sleeping bodies. His skin tightened. The age spots vanished. The wrinkles smoothed. His muscles became more defined, his hair thicker, the grey disappeared. Daishuku was getting younger.

When the morning staff took over, they found his clothes sagged, the area bereft of a body, his blanket crumpled over the fleeting sights of Mae, a large, bright, blinding cavity in the floor, which felt a little like looking at the sun.

Backwards into the chasm. Here. Daishuku was twenty-five, walking through acres of cornfield. The tips of tall stalks bent in the breeze, the thin sticks planted beside them on either side a guard to stop the winds wreaking havoc. The corn when it grew as expected was sweet, ripened from the dew and rain and good intentions, from Daishuku tending his father's land in the heat, under downpours, when the cold made his hands gnarled. At the edge of the land stood a bamboo house, a bamboo house with insect legs planted in the ground in a precarious union, where the outcome was a possible uprooting into the skyline or collapsing from baskets of corn piled on the small porch, the empty chair where his mother used to sew becoming a pit stop for the grey cat leisurely trailing invisible small territories. Daishuku tugged the hoe over his shoulders, his footsteps quickening, his left arm pushing the weight of stalks away, like malleable green curtains the land coughed up. His fingers knew the softness of the soil, its dusky hue, the measure of water on the stalks, the shafts of light falling through, the sharp, occasional thin cuts, the tiny bulbs of blood like stagnant ladybirds waiting for permission to move. The bamboo house trembled. He paused, listening, heard the crinkle of a straw mat, a cream puddle in one path. He listened for Mae the bruised Murasaki Shikibu to press her petals against the blade of his hoe.

He heard the swoosh of stalks pushed back, a wrinkling amid a sea of green, the air cool on his neck as his body went into alert mode just in case. He stepped to the side, obscured by some stalks, his grip tightening on the hoe. The small scar from an incision on the inside of his left wrist itched. He resisted the urge to scratch it, taking deep breaths instead. In the distance, the door of the bamboo house flung open, shuddering as the costumes of previous occupants crinkled in the doorway. The gentle patter of footsteps approached, then a whistling sound, their signal. He smiled, relieved. A rush of warmth heated his skin, stirring him inside. He dropped the hoe, stepped back into the line of vision. Mae appeared, a sheepish expression on her face. Her slender frame belied a toughness that slowly revealed itself. Her dented, stubborn chin, high forehead, slash of curved mouth spoke of an unconventional beauty. Her dark, silky knot of hair was tucked underneath a wide straw hat. Dressed like a man in her slightly baggy, black Haori suit, she carried a rolled-up mat tucked beneath one arm, a small bag of sliced oranges in the other, the juice like a burst artery of sweet nectar. She spread the mat on the floor, took off her hat. *If only our warring fathers could see the resolution to a small war can come through the children.*

Daishuku laughed. Mae was prone to random

philosophical musings he found oddly endearing. He was less naïve.

Their fathers hated each other too and the men who came before them, he said.

They lay down, the sway and bending of stalks a lullaby. She fed him two slices of orange; he licked her fingers, making a popping sound, which amused her. Her shirt flapped against her stomach, a pouch hidden by baggy clothing. He pressed his hand there for kicks that were yet to come. Looking beyond them, he imagined Mae's stomach rising through the green, expanding, anchored by his hand. The tips of stalks snapped around them. He listened for the sound of a grain of corn in a growing tiny fist. Mae kissed his wrist, promised to insert the orange pips in his incision so she could watch them bloom into fruit that would distort in quiet spaces.

The cat on the bamboo porch separated into parts. The costumes worshipped a stalk growing from a crack in the doorway, christened with a thick line of orange dew.

The war between the two families began generations back over land when their great-grandfathers had been best friends. The land that bordered Niigata was at least four hundred acres, had an apple orchard, a run of chicken houses, a well, a saw mill. An emperor's son had gifted it to Daishuku's great-grandfather, Hiroku, for intercepting and saving his life one night on a dangerous road when two bandits ambushed him. Hiroku had in turn told Akira, Mae's great-grandfather, about his new small fortune. A promise was made, a handshake exchanged, a plan to toil on that land together, to yield its fruit to build an inheritance for their families. But Hiroku was a gambler, a drunkard.

He could often be spotted stumbling from the gambling houses, clothes dishevelled, reeking of sake, mumbling about his ancestors, his wife's continuous lack of interest in him, the unpredictable behaviour of his children, a streak of recklessness he wrestled with, particularly appearing in the men of his lineage. It skipped the odd one here and there but nevertheless reared its head eventually. It was rumoured Hiroku owed several debts. They mounted, one on top of the other. Great stone burdens that dented his shoulders, changed his once-proud walk.

One night, high on sake and false confidence, he gambled the emperor's gift away.

He cried all the way home, drunkenly waving his arms like a windmill's interpretation of a panicked man. At home, he broke the news to his wife Azumi who, glowering in anger, threatened to cut his body into little pieces, then dump them in the well they'd never drink from. His children grew to resent him for the loss of their inheritance. When the news travelled, a furious Akira vowed never to speak to his old friend again. And so a rift occurred between the clans; a rip that expanded, gathering blood clouds in its wake. Hiroku continued to drink. Azumi became a stranger in his bed. The children grew. The years passed. His friend Akira never reneged on his promise. In their seventies, their hair whitened, bodies stooped over canes, words slow from their tongues, one cold night Akira saw a heart bleeding on his bed mat. Thinking his old eyes were playing tricks, he poked it with his cane. The heart dodged the poking, rolling away into the night.

The next week, Hiroku died of a heart attack, pieces of his heart scattering in the rift.

On the evening of his twentieth birthday, Daishuku headed to his family's outhouse clutching a lantern, a task he'd become accustomed to since the incidence of bandit raids increased over the month. They thrived on the highways of Honshū, catching wealthy travellers passing through off guard. They weren't killers but nevertheless used coercion, the threat of violence to terrify their victims. The notorious Paniko gang even struck homes on the outskirts. Families were on alert. The squeaking of the lantern slowly swaying in his hand merged with the soft whispers of the corn-stalks. In the preceding two weeks, Daishuku had noticed items missing from the outhouse: a beautiful golden fan, a wooden tobacco case bearing a dragon's motif, an ancient Sho. A creaking sound in the outhouse pricked his ears. He heard rummaging, then stillness, as if the intruder had anticipated his approach. After the awkwardness of ado-lescence, he'd blossomed. He was above average height, with elegantly handsome features, which belied what most would consider a lower social status as a farmer's son. Thick, expressive brows often gave the impression that he was scowling when deep in thought. His long hair was piled into a loose topknot. He set the lantern down carefully, waiting calmly, aware of the pocket knife strapped to his ankle should he need it. He kicked the door open. The thwack jolted the assailant who spun round.

You must be a weaker strain of the Paniko, sent to rob chicken houses and the vulnerable, Daishuku said, by way of greeting.

Dressed in black, topped off with a Sugegasa hat, the assailant flew at him. He was slighter than Daishuku expected, though fast and agile. They wrestled on the ground. Amid the flailing of arms and blocking of punches, Daishuku stopped. He was certain his chest had brushed against breasts.

Be still! he instructed, pinning the intruder down by the shoulders. He removed their hat. Midnight hair cascaded down. A choppy fringe, restless brown eyes were revealed. There were dirt marks on her face, plus an expression of deep annoyance, mouth curved into a sneer. He stood up, stepped back, his body humming as recognition hit him. *You are Kitamo's daughter.*

She scrambled to her feet, brushing the dust off her clothes. *Yes. Congratulations. The dunce gene skipped you. And you are Makoto's son. Stay back, peasant! Before I gut you like a meal from the Tenryū river,* she warned, rolling her sleeves up, hand clenched into fists.

What exactly is the Paniko's ideology? What is in the manifesto, if you have one? Or is it just a front for directionless opportunists? Daishuku mused, walking back towards the doorway, blocking her exit.

Halfwit, the Paniko run these regions! Soon, we'll have government officials right where we want them, she spat, walking towards him, fishing out a folded sheaf of weathered brown paper from her chest, bearing scribbling on the back: a map, which had England circled in red. She held it up to him as though it was a challenge.

He snatched it from her. *Ah, you plan to extend your thieving beyond these territories,* he said, bemused. Her nostrils flared.

She pointed at the map's red circle, the creases formed, gathered like the lines of a sleeping storm. *One day, I will travel there. I will build things you can't imagine while you are here drinking sake with goats! Becoming the worst version of your ancestor.*

He grabbed her arm, steering her outside. *Come again,* he added, holding her gaze, daring her to. Then Mae the bandit woman was running through the cornfield, light from the lantern a waning orb. Her hair trailing behind was a raven's abandoned wing; her lips pursed over his pocket knife like a bit between her teeth.

*

Backwards into the lacuna. Here he was ten, accompanying his father, Makoto, to make his round of deliveries in the town centre. He sat on the stoop of a shop, which sold carved wooden shoes that looked like small ships, an old Shakuhachi instrument, a green glass bowl twinkling at the rim, large maps of places he'd never heard his father mention. He pointed to one hanging map. He saw the figure of a small girl crossing the miniature-shaped countries. She held a dagger, waving it from side to side at a crinkled sun, which loomed at the edge. The sun shrank. The girl's hands faded. The dagger spun, the countries rearranged themselves. The girl disappeared. He waved the store owner over, his finger jabbing at the map, which felt smooth beneath his touch. The old man, who wore an eye glass, slapped Daishuku's fingers away, peered at the map, saw nothing. He didn't know it then but Daishuku had witnessed the strands of time colliding. The store owner gave him a sweet to stop his hands wandering. He ran back outside, searching for his father in the stream of people milling about, wondering who the girl from the map was, sucking the soft-centred black sweet, unaware of the bright liquid seeping into the roof of his mouth. The street swirled. The sound of a car engine revving caught his attention. He ran towards it, a brown beetle that reminded him of a giant locust. The man at the wheel lit a stick of tobacco, rolled the window down. On the dashboard were two dice pieces, a wilted purple furan, a box of matches. The scrawny man drummed his fingers against the wheel as he smoked, waiting. Daishuku slowed down passing the car, guided by an instinct that made his stomach tumble. His skin tingled. A lump in his throat formed. He passed the women dyeing cloths in buckets before wringing them, determinedly twisting the material as if they'd crawl away from their clutches, like dyed, hand-spun cobras. He wandered through the smoke, the sizzle of street food cooking in large woks, the men and women stirring, wiping their brows, negotiating with hagglers. The scent of spicy Sukiyaki lingered in the air. He spotted his father in a damp alleyway behind the rubber factory, arguing with a man in a silken, cream suit. The man held a bowl of Miyabi soup in his right hand. The scene seemed unsteady somehow, as if a ripple in the ground would cave their footing. His father's expression was drawn, his shoulders slumped. Steam blew from the factory pipes, like a smokescreen. The man waved his fist in his father's face. His father shrank back. Then the man's face paled. The bowl fell from his hand. The soup spilled. The chopsticks clattered to the ground. His father ran, almost knocking into him at the entrance. Daishuku gasped from the impact. His father picked him up, instructing him to be quiet as he ran. This was the closest he could remember them being, his father holding him in flight.

The man stumbled out of the alleyway to the waiting beetle, clambered in. The engine revved once more. Daishuku looked beyond his father's shoulders at people swarming, separating into clusters, like a symphony the engine had accidentally set off. The sound began to thin as though marooned on a distant shore. Soon enough, his weight became too much for his father's arms. Their hearts beating almost simultaneously, he watched for the alleyway's steam to deliver dice and a dead furan into their route of escape.

Daishuku watched the policemen approaching their home from a distance, on the bend, like uniformed ants, getting closer and closer, their proudly pressed uniforms lightly covered with dust, the gold buttons like shrunken badges catching the shattered ends of a fallow summer. The stiffened uniforms were stretched tautly over their bodies, as if they'd abandon the figures, leave them naked, the uniforms walking through whispering corn in a separate ambush. For days, the stalks had shivered in warning, their tips grazing each other in collusion, rust crawling up the tassels. And a withered reflection sucking from the rust till blind, till mired in the soil, the dirt, in the minuscule grains trying to morph into a valve; a release.

Daishuku ran to get Makoto, who'd lost his appetite for days, whose reflections wandered through their home trying to eat slivers of light on his behalf. Standing by the window with his father, Daishuku pointed at the soldiers. His mother, Reiko, emerged from the mat in their bedroom screaming, asking Makoto what shame he'd brought on the family. Her face whitened. Crestfallen, she splintered. Hundreds of her heads were shrieking in the stalks. Her kimono gown multiplied, burrowing in the soil in search of roots to mimic. Daishuku covered his ears; his heart was beating so fast he thought his chest would crack open. He looked to his parents for reassurance but each was unravelling. He knew that moment would change everything. He just couldn't understand how. Almost in a stupor, his father, Makoto, walked slowly to the front doorway. The policemen came. They dragged Makoto to the ground, on his knees; Reiko cried, circling uncontrollably. Powerless, Daishuku ran to Makoto, a bruised boy desperately trying to grab his father's hand one last time.

He stood at the edge of the bamboo house. A broken siren became a fold of sleep.

Makoto had poisoned a man to whom he owed a great debt.

The bamboo house collapsed.

Backwards into the current. Here. Daishuku was a tiny sperm curling, darting, shooting. Flanked by a flood of scenes that were small membranes finding their elasticity. The scenes attempted to keep up but they were loaded with concoctions of pain and joy and longing, the results of which were little erosions, a caving here or there, a withering at the tip, holes off centre a finger could slip through, a dribble of ink, the lines of a small country. The membranes beat in the current, limped along obediently, bound by barely visible threads glimmering occasionally. Speeding, the sperm was ahead, sharply turning, twisting, gathering momentum, a white tadpole drunk on its own movement. Unaware that, one day, it would be a man who'd fall in love with a woman called Mae, who'd carry a stalk in her mouth to England, who'd give him a son there. And that the son would follow the root of the stalk back to Japan, only to go missing clutching his father's dagger, like a last lifeline. Mae, the mother, would die of a broken heart, the father would never recover from her loss.

Upstream, the sperm encountered memories it would claim in the future, memories that waited patiently to deceive it, to present themselves as voids, rearrange components on cold city streets, underpasses, in borrowed clothing that collapsed into puddles of colour, into folded points between dimensions and as reflections mirrored in oil spills. Shooting forward, the sperm continued on its destined trail.

It was a piece of glass in the vein, a spot of blood travelling through a season of snow, a musical chord colliding with an infant's silhouette.

Daishuku was beginning again: a slither rumbling the boughs, rupturing a haze of memories and membranes. Heading for the cold womb precariously balanced on a curb, flooded with water, light, and the angles of several resurrections.

Mangata

The man who brought a miracle to the small town in northern Mozambique was both remarkable and ordinary. As an albino, he wasn't an unfamiliar sight although other things indicated he was different: he walked with a certain comfort in his skin that wasn't of the surroundings; assured, confident. He had a birthmark on his neck, which looked like a stem growing from his movements. His nails were painted black, his hands elegant, the fingers long, tapered. His tongue sported a silver ring at the tip, a pink, pierced entity darting out readily to abandon his mouth. On the afternoon Terry Midas arrived, it was scorching.

He stood waiting at the pick-up point near the market, a black god painted alabaster holding his light travel bag. His batik shirt had sweat patches; tan trousers stuck to his clammy thighs uncomfortably. The dust-covered leather sandals he wore felt heavy, he having walked a few miles in the bush to get to this point. He'd done so with trepidation, fear scattering wildfire into his veins as it spread through his limbs. He knew the stories of albinos being persecuted, hunted for the value of their body parts, kidnapped, killed and sold. During the walk, in his mind's eye he'd seen flashes of cutlasses raised up, bones on the necks of men whispering in the voices of ancestors. The cries of medicine men splintered in his ears. He'd seen blood in the sky and the trees shedding pale skin. He'd arrived at the market gratefully, spat from the torturous bush, out of breath. Ten years away and nothing had prepared him for the intensity of being back, the heat, the dusty roads, the shanty houses made quaint by the distance of separation, the slick black bodies rhapsodic in their freedom. He hadn't been primed for the warmth, small bursts of joy, the fear, the feeling of familiarity, the feeling of being foreign, a mouthful of echoes slipping teasingly out of reach. Sweating profusely, he stood, walked to a shaded corner of the shop he'd decided to wait at, thinking of albinos that had appeared to him through night traffic; hundreds of them, each holding angles of light doubling as rabbit holes. It came to him then, the memory of that night years ago. The thick, suffocating heat, sluggish grasshoppers chorusing, mosquitoes hovering around the one stubby shrinking candle in their shack as if drawn to a possible death. Mama Carlos sat snoozing gently by the door to protect him in a ritual that saw her bloodshot eyes close reluctantly, eventually succumbing to the demands of the body, her large bosom rising steadily up and down. The small picture of Christ pinned on the wall above the green mosquito net, which swooped down, tiny winged fireflies with far too much gumption zigzagging above their heads. And Christ's robes singed from the blue candle flame that thought it could fly, bending wilfully in the heat, his eyes temporarily blinded by tiny bloodshot figures taking residence there.

Terry on the bed, tossing and turning, the sound of water in the empty petrol can on the floor by his pillow of bunched clothes. Then three men kicked down their door. He saw the glint of blades at Mama Carlos's throat, heard rough, urgent orders being issued, Mama Carlos screaming so loudly their response was a backhand slap to her face. Terry shrank back against the wall, powerless, pale and trembling. Necklaces of small bones on the men's necks jangled, their faces partially obscured by handkerchiefs tied over their mouths. The smell of the day's sweat from their bodies mingled with fear in the room was potent. They dragged him to the rusted white truck outside, dumped him in the back, then piled in laughing, the truck screeching away, exhaust-pipe smoke curling around the edges of an abduction. They sped off; the truck eventually wound its way around the bush. It was at this point Terry leaped out, running for his life. He ran so fast blindly, an alabaster boy slipped from the world's pocket into the night's cruel playground. He ignored the scratches of wild plants on his legs, the stinging on his arms. The men had left the truck, whistling crudely, clicking their fingers to catch him again.

A path snaked through the bush, appearing from nowhere, glimmering. Rising, rushing, similar to the noise made in their petrol can at home. He ran along the path. He never remembered how he got all the way back to the village. He'd cried in relief at the people gathered holding kerosene lamps, babbling at them frantically, half out of his mind and skin. And everything being in the wrong place: their shack uprooted from Mama Carlos's injuries, the girl who'd given him a green banana earlier in the day balancing a basket of bones instead on her head, clicking her fingers, Christ's photo tearing through the route of the truck, his face covered with a soiled handkerchief, Mama Carlos screaming into the petrol can, the candle flame growing into a blue-tongued carcass in the bush. And the lines of the night reduced into the shape of a howl beneath tyres crunching on stones.

Terry pulled a cigarette from his pocket, lit it and took a drag. *Get a hold of yourself*, he thought. Six years in New York followed by four in London working for one of the best architectural firms had cemented his desire to build houses that were unusual living experiences: a mountain lodge in Shanghai; homes in the Arctic, communal buildings in Abu Dhabi; eco lodges in the untamed Madagascar forest. His experiences of extreme weather, ice and heat confirmed just how tiny humans are, at the mercy of the elements, the unexpected. He knew those feelings of fear and anxiety. He'd run from them only to find they had taken root in him anyway. Once he'd dated a fire-eater from Guinea Bissau whose skin he imagined tasted of flammable liquids, whose pliable mouth parted pleasurably walking barefoot through compact tracks of fire in her garden. Their mutual dysfunction had worked for a while until one day he saw her in her bedroom doorway, head engulfed in flames holding a familiar petrol can, the bedroom transformed into a bush that couldn't be contained, shooting rapidly towards the ceiling till he couldn't breathe. There were small lit creatures wailing, leaping from her fire head through the window to change guises in a distant Mozambican night.

Terry took another pull from the cigarette. His desire to build had brought him home, this time for a smaller project: water fountains in the town and village.

The years had passed but he hadn't forgotten that for albinos like him, the simple, natural, instinctive act of seeking water could kill you.

Four years ago, Mama Carlos had died in her sleep of natural causes. The medicine men said her luck had run out. If albinos were hunted for the good fortune they were meant to bring, her one major contribution to the Midas family lineage, birthing an albino son, had brought her nothing but heartache and devastation. Nobody knew who Terry's father was. Marguerite Carlos was a stout, large-bosomed woman of average looks. She possessed a bawdy rumble of laughter that got into your system, a certain mischief, a curiosity in her gaze beyond the simple woman she appeared to be. She was a street vendor who sold bean cakes; stewed handfuls of delicious, spicy rice wrapped in parcels of broad leaves; caramelised sweets the shape of umbrellas.

Thirty-one years ago, after an evening of selling on one of the main roads, she returned to the village temporarily blind. The light in her eyes had shattered into something distant. She babbled to other villagers about an immaculate conception; the virgin blood running down her thighs watered grateful patches of weathered ground. Her flowery white blouse was torn, a large bruise on her neck reddening. Her wares had been left on the road; the silver tray clattered to the ground having caught the reflection of a number of ventriloquist hands in a pale costume; her bean cakes split, then crumbled. The umbrella sweets melted into stubs of colour, packets of rice unfolded; tiny offerings to vehicles flying past, an occasional hungry god, a wayward shadow. Marguerite fled the roadside, cicadas crying in her eardrums. The night receded into an unruly trinity of miracle, virgin blood and fractured light. Marguerite's sight returned when Terry was born.

He'd just fallen off an oil rig in the Atlantic Ocean when he knew she was dead. He'd felt a missile pass through his chest into the water. Slick like a seal caught in greasy spillage, he'd looked up at the endless stretches of sky, his head full of cloud blue silence. He could barely move. The weight of her death had cracked him. Four years of gifts made of smoke vanishing in his pockets. Four years of shimmering angles of water undulating in mirrors he passed. He'd had to come home.

He checked his watch. It was after 3.30 p.m.; still no pick-up. He sighed, feeling some tension leave his body. The area around him swam. A man whistled on his bicycle riding by, a bundle of gold-coloured traditional cloth in the small basket compartment. Another man wearing a white vest sat by the entrance of the barbershop opposite, slicing a watermelon open with a cutlass, its damp pink insides exposed. An emaciated dog ambled past leisurely, tongue dangling, as if poised to trace the shadows of passers-by. It sat at the barbershop stoop by the cutlass on the floor. The man stroked its ears, glaring at Terry. Terry nodded in greeting just as another man in a New York Yankees hat passed on the dusty path holding two dead, plucked fowls tied together at the ankles with a piece of white string, broken daylight trapped in their still eyes. The dog rose, laughter, music and the clink of bottles filtered through from the barbershop. One barber appeared at the netted window holding a clipper; he raised his other hand in greeting. People had begun to notice him but there was no recognition. He'd expected that, after all this time. Streams of people wandered past. He was so lost in his reverie he barely noticed a cluster of albino children had gathered, until one boy raised Terry's wallet into the air, a worn five-pound note held in victory accompanying the boy's dimpled smile. 'Mr Money-maker! If you let me keep this proper British money, I will give you your wallet back.'

Terry hadn't felt the wallet being slipped from his pocket. The small gang of pickpockets watched his face expectantly. He saw himself reflected in their pale skin, their African features, searching eyes. Little versions of himself scurrying around in the heat up to God knew what. Something dissolved inside him.

His voice was calm, measured. 'I'm waiting for Gonzalez to pick me up. You know him?' He was even more aware of his accent, New York via London. How odd he must have appeared to them. The group fell upon each other laughing, an unplanned chorus of joy.

'Ah, mister, you don't know anything!' the thief said, dimples deepening. 'Gonzalez starts drinking from one o'clock! You will be waiting here till next week. We take you where you want to go. Come.' Cheekily, the boy handed only the wallet back. Before Terry knew it, they'd surrounded him. Another boy grabbed his travel bag. A third boy offered him a half-eaten chocolate bar. He accepted, popping it into his mouth as that boy steered him forward. He followed them, his gut instinct taking over. The only girl in the group twirled a stick expertly, like a baton, in her right hand, Terry's white handkerchief fashioned into a headband on her braided hair, which brushed her shoulders. She shot ahead of them as though used to disrupting the order of things.

'Mister, what did you bring for me from abroad?' she cooed.

They referred to each other by nickname. One by one, who was who cemented in Terry's brain. Molanko, the Duke of Hazards, was the trickster who'd pilfered his wallet. Kwashoko Joe with the protruding stomach had given him the piece of chocolate. He was the group's go-to man for sweets and other edible spoils. Upright Moses was the one with the stammer. And the girl, Whitney Houston, had been ironically nicknamed because she loved to sing, badly, warbling tunes that would have given a cat wailing in Hades a run for its money, unwittingly making songs unrecognisable. They talked non-stop. They knew which routes to get where, who to speak to about any transactions, who'd fallen out with whom, who was new in the village. They talked affectionately about Bathsheba Tavares, the school teacher living in his mother's house. Terry realised these eleven-year-old street hustlers could be his eyes and ears on the ground. He thought back to his pit stop at the handful of shops, the man with the cutlass's unwelcoming gaze lingering on his skin as if assessing its worth. A knot of fear formed in his stomach as the children walked him through the outskirts of the village. He thought of that dog drinking from his redemption in a watery night, the man on the bicycle unable to climb off, the fowls in the basket compartment instead, dressed in the bright, native material, raising their stilted gazes to trap items that would reveal themselves as sly weapons. The sound of the cutlass striking was silent as the watermelon split again, white string from the fowls' ankles tugging a miniature damp scene from the watermelon's pink innards. Terry struggled to identify the images. He raised his head to watch the ruins of himself gleaming on the rusted aluminium roof-tops of homes they passed.

The children left him at the door, promising to find him the next day. He watched them leaving, becoming smaller in the distance, their peals of laughter swallowed by an evening mirage. They were pre-pubescent bodies in street costumes he knew wouldn't prepare them for the devasta-tions to come. His stomach rumbled. His eyes took in the house: a small, ramshackle yellow bungalow. It overlooked a street lined with similar homes; a drooping plant sat on the cracked window sill. The netted wooden door was open. He stepped inside, half expecting Mama Carlos to be snoozing gently or filling those broad leaves with the alchemy of ingredients, a comforting ritual he remembered from childhood. Instead he walked through the short hall-way area into a rustic living room. A fan whirred steadily on a side table; beside it lay a weathered copy of Anaïs Nin's *Delta of Venus*. In the middle stood an old green sofa covered with a warm-coloured patterned throw. On the opposite side was another table, with miniature red clay

figures bearing eerily human-like expressions surrounding
an atlas that had pins stuck in various countries. One black-
and-white photograph of a young Miriam Makeba hung
on the wall. A sharp pain flooded his chest. Signs of living
that weren't his mother's. The sound of a drill interrupted
the fan's quiet symphony. He followed it, past three other
rooms, a bathroom and toilet, through the kitchen area
and out to a workshop space where a woman was drilling
holes into a block of wood. She uncurled rather than stood,
drill in hand, shaved head, skin so dark and rich to be the
opposite of his. A slash of cheekbones, wide, full mouth;
native tribal tattoos crawled up her left arm. Roughly five
foot four, she wore faded blue dungarees over a Steve Biko
T-shirt. She switched the drill off, lifted the goggles from
her face to reveal amused, slanted eyes. 'You came home,'
she said, as if conversations needn't start with introduc-
tions. 'After paying you rent for this long, I wondered
when you'd come to check on your tenant. Your mother
never stopped talking about you.' Her throat constricted as
though she'd caught something fleeting in there. A trickle
of sweat ran down her neck. He resented her empathy. He
resented the way she looked at him like she knew him.
What he was thinking was, were it possible, he wanted to
bury his dick into her gleaming head and drink from her
collarbone. He wondered how his moment of grief had been
intercepted by desire, by his body's betrayal.

'What kind of African woman is called Bathsheba? I

could have been anybody. You should be more careful. Don't leave that door open,' he remarked. He'd never been good at small-talk. He didn't see a reason to start.

She uttered something in Portuguese, flicked the drill on. In his peripheral vision, the atlas split against the drill, leaving both of them to scramble for pieces of that world later. The twist drill came off, tumbling in his blood, scouring for a root buried so deeply it'd surely become part of his DNA.

She slipped the goggles back on. 'You can have the bigger room,' she offered. 'What kind of man misses his mother's funeral?' she asked, mouth a flat line.

'I'll take the bigger room. It's my house after all,' he answered, already turning his back, crossing into the kitchen. The click of his sandals faded between them.

He knew the room had been Mama Carlos's. The worn brown slippers under the dipping bed were roughly her size; a figurine of two angels praying rested at the edge of an old dresser. In the wardrobe, some of her clothes were folded at the bottom left corner. A few hangers beckoned on the wardrobe's metallic rod, bare carcasses of her life.

He took his sandals off, the soft blue mat beneath his feet a welcome relief after the day's heaviness. He unpacked slowly, the simple task rooting him. He'd packed lightly: a few T-shirts, shorts, a couple of pairs of trousers, a light felt hat he'd bought in Panama, a pair of dark blue Missoni sunglasses.

At thirteen, Terry had become obsessed with an albino man named Juan Cardoza, who came to their village to see his cousin Benedito. Juan was tall and sophisticated; he wore pastel-coloured linen suits and sunglasses from abroad. He was casually cool about everything, never in a rush, bending the world to his pace instead. Terry had been convinced this man was his father. He was a similar age to Mama Carlos, went out of his way to buy items from her. He possessed a worldly air. Terry discreetly took to following him, to the local bar, at the market, to football games, until Juan had reported him to Mama Carlos, worried his behaviour was unhealthy. Terry had burned with shame at the time. Juan returned to Maputo a few weeks later but Terry never forgot him or the possibilities he'd presented.

He took his shirt off, sat on the bed. His shoulders heaved as the sound of Bathsheba's drill reverberated in the silence. He cried quietly. He'd forgotten that being in Mozambique, being home, could bring those sleeping memories hurtling to the surface, awake, ready to be fed. The wardrobe door flew open, creaking. He half expected other memories to limp out towards the angels' figurine to reveal their secrets while the figurine listened patiently before falling off the edge. Soon, the delivery of fountain parts would arrive. He could get on with what he'd come home to do. Thank God.

*

He put the word out through barbers in the town that he was seeking labour to install fountains locally. He knew it was dangerous but he didn't want to get in outside contractors, which would have defeated the whole purpose. He believed in sourcing local talent, handing them a blueprint of being autonomous, watching the idea of potential assemble into curious, light-filled shapes in their eyes. He'd trialled a similar project in a Soweto township several years back. A generous venture capitalist had provided the funding then. This was his money. His risk to take. More importantly, it was Mama Carlos's home. The place where blue-flamed carcasses fragmented into pieces taking refuge in kerosene lamps. Maybe it was the heat, the dusty earth he walked barefoot in outside the house, but he felt his insides upended every day. As if his organs were tied to strings that had unravelled, untethered, parts of him hovering in a darkness blind to external traffic. He woke up on a few occasions worried he'd find his lung shrinking in the bedroom doorway, his liver spinning into shreds at the edge of Bathsheba's drill while her plump mouth opened, his heart frantically beating on the living-room table, the clay figures rushing towards it as though it was a troubled sun.

In the end, he employed twenty men; at least sixty had expressed interest. When the truck of fountain parts and tools arrived, tearing through the dust into the town centre, the men gathered round excitedly. They offloaded everything, carrying the curved white ceramic bowls like silent children. Work began a day later. Twenty fountains to be installed in key areas. Somehow the children always found him, those mini reflections of himself, Molanko, Kwashoko Joe, Upright Moses and Whitney Houston, hovering around activities to learn or perhaps keep an eye on him in an unspoken show of loyalty. Asking question after question:

Mr Terry, can you fly an aeroplane?

Next time will you bring champagne from London?

Mr Terry, I want to play for Manchester United. Do you know the manager?

Mr Terry, can you take us to London?

Mr Terry, Mr Terry, Mr Terry. His name trilled on their lips in hymn-like fashion. Terry oversaw the installations, often working himself, unaware that at least one of his workers had a horn-shaped pale bone buried in his pocket.

Terry imagined water springing from the fountains, bursting from every part of the town's crevice; the cleanness of it, the new beginnings in its malleable lines, the resurrection it provided, trickling, rushing, circling. He saw it all, the way he had in his dreams. The way he had in his nightmares.

Over the next three weeks the fountains were installed in various areas: outside a school, by the market where throngs of people wound their way noisily through come market day three days a week, beside a large, patchy field that doubled as a football ground, where tournaments were managed by the local mechanic who happened to have been a talented footballer in his youth. There was a fountain in the bus depot area at the town's centre, outside the general hospital, by the building where community leaders met for gatherings. They were dotted around, curved, pale and inviting, ready for water to trickle through.

Terry developed camaraderie with his group of workers. During breaks, he'd buy them street food. They gathered in clusters eating, drinking bitter lemon and beer, sharing the day's stories, mutated fevers that captured them flanked by empty bottles, crushed Guinness cans catching the day's memories, like stray capsules. He enjoyed these moments. They temporarily sated his loneliness, slowed the feeling of unravelling. And provided a counter to his and Bathsheba's circling of each other at the house, he trying to contain the broken pieces of himself, she constantly crafting small things.

Three weeks later, the jobs were done. The workers were no longer needed. The water didn't trickle through the fountains. The pipes were faulty, some blocked. Word spread that the albino man from abroad had brought the town bad luck. The fountains, physical manifestations of Terry's good intentions, stood mockingly, ceramic visions gathering dust. For a week he felt adrift, frustrated that his plans had ground to a halt. He waited for a sign, a solution from beyond the grave sent by Mama Carlos.

*

It was an intensely hot afternoon the day the children accosted him in town. Molanko and the crew had left school early to find him. Terry had just got his hair cut at the barber's when he spotted them. He stood outside the barbershop, popped a stick of gum in his mouth. He waved them over half smiling. His shades were tucked into the pocket on his white cotton shirt. He patted his trouser pocket to ensure his wallet was there. He was glad to escape the shop, away from the eyes of men who watched him like an organism growing beyond the confines of a Petri dish. Their false laughter grated on him, their silent, exchanged looks a shared communication with a menacing edge. He'd watched them back discreetly, worried his reflection would abandon the mirror, half-shorn head and broken bits of artificial light in tow, to take its chances with the perils of the afternoon.

Molanko ran to him, a Public Enemy record tucked under his arm, its weathered sleeve exposed. 'I found it! It is mine,' he declared, standing beside Terry decisively as if that would add weight to his statement.

'Selfish Judas!' Kwashoko Joe accused, flying at him then attempting to yank the record from his hands. 'It was my idea to go to Papa Joe's so half is mine.'

'J-j-j-just break it into two then nobody can p-p-play it.' Upright Moses stammered his contribution.

Whitney Houston, in a yellow dress at least two sizes too large, said, 'Public Enemy cannot even sing.' She missed the irony of her comment, eyes homing in on Terry's Missoni shades instead.

'Quiet, give it to me.' Terry instructed, niftily grabbing the record. 'Let's go.'

They went scavenging for discarded items. They built and improvised instruments. Upright Moses used a whistle, Whitney Houston old tomato cans with stones inside. Kwashoko Joe played a damaged flute. Molanko, never one to be outdone, built a makeshift guitar from a calabash bowl, a bed headboard stick and strings. They played on the football field, free of watchful eyes and judgement, liberated. Terry rapped. He taught them verses of Public Enemy's 'Fight the Power'. And Whitney Houston in her yellow dress, white hair cornrowed into pigtails, displaying the quickest lyrical delivery, triumphantly wearing Terry's Missoni shades, was a born star after all, dancing on the pale lines of the field.

After Terry dropped the children off safely, the air was denser on his way home. He heard scurrying in the trees. A sliver of sweat ran down his back. A molten creature left its teeth-marks in his veins. His increased heart rate distorted the skyline. It was faint but he heard it drawing closer, twisting in the air, a transparent boomerang that knew its target. It was the sound of broken bones jangling as necklaces, travelling through a blue road in the sky, collapsing to reappear as a dawn.

He picked up the pace, worried by the rapid appearances of shadows sent by bodies in the wings to track him. And in the gaps between twitching tree branches, the outlines of constellations encountered the angles of cutlass blades.

That night he sat up in bed, feeling the call of the bush taunting him to collect what he'd lost there all those years ago. He knew he owed it a debt. He sensed the movements of its inhabitants passing through his limbs, misshapen by the lost parts of painful memories. He got up, washed his face. He rapped on Bathsheba's door. She answered after five knocks dressed in a Road Runner T-shirt and blue denim shorts. Her hands were covered with red clay. She held a napkin. Her head gleamed, a rare fruit that appeared in doorways, in the low rumblings of possibilities.

'Hey, you came just when I needed an interruption,' she said, wiping her hands.

His tongue felt weighty, spawned from a desert.

He rocked on his heels. 'I like the shape of your head, your mouth. I want to know those parts of you. You say so much with very little. You keep ... making things. It's distracting, attractive. I'm your landlord.'

'We've already established that.' She laughed, stepped aside. He walked in. Her room smelt of incense. A half-built red clay man lay on the bedside table on a piece of cardboard, waiting to be fully formed. Restless, he didn't sit.

'I failed,' he said, watching to see the confirmation in her expression.

She dropped the napkin by the little clay man. 'No, you made people feel like they matter. It's a quality visionary men have. They carry people along, give them the sense that anything's possible. Marguerite always said you'd do something unexpected. You're full of intent. My God, you look so—'

'Strange?' he finished, a note of irritability in his tone.

She inched closer. 'Other-worldly, strangely beautiful. It's hard not to keep looking at you.' She pressed her lips against the pulse in his neck, then a finger to steady it. As if she'd known its rhythm long before he came to her.

As her mouth continued its assured exploration of his body, he closed his eyes feeling her red fingerprints on his skin. He couldn't tell where his limbs, the bed, the earth all began and ended, somehow intertwined. The heat thickened. The ceiling became ash, memory a one-hoofed present, past a baby in search of a dusty, distended nipple. A blue carcass hovered near the bed; the moon became an overgrown yolk; the studded blackened sky folded into itself; the night shrieked.

Bathsheba awoke the next morning to the heavy, thunderous sound of rain, to an empty space in her bed. Naked, she threw on a T-shirt, three-quarter-length black trousers, sandals. Instinctively she knew Terry wasn't in the house.

She walked out to find deep, endless stretches of glinting silver water. Foil-coloured, shiny. Silver rain kept falling. It had flooded the town overnight. Her heart rate increased. She had to find Terry. She needed to tell him the arrival of his fountains had caused something remarkable to happen. She waded through waist-deep waters in shock. Uprooted houses floated, shops had collapsed, people made their way dripping artificial like rivulets, holding belongings on their heads, bodies submerged in a liquid morning. It was devastating, miraculous, silver water in a forgotten town. There were miles and miles of it undulating, spreading, covering, rising. Cars became sunken submarines, water gushing from their doors.

And the children, Molanko, the Duke of Hazards, Upright Moses, Kwashoko Joe and Whitney Houston, were transported by the waters, carried along clutching their handmade instruments all the way to the bush. Emerging transformed into glimmering small gods, offering their instruments to the only remaining body part of Terry Midas: his birthmarked neck pinned on a stick as a trophy high above the gnarling wild brushes, spilling silver water in the aftermath of something born from a severing.

Komza Bright Morning

She doesn't tell me her real name.

Real names, she says, *are for the misguided, people who want to be locked in. That's not me. I'm metal melted down. I'm a needle in the blood looking for an eye. My threads could come from anywhere. I'm Muhammad wearing the mountain's clothes. You look wayward, baby, lost. Are you James Baldwin seeking his Paris? Or are you Josephine Baker? Paris is in Paris. This is Berlin.*

He or she or however she identifies: transsexual? Pansexual? Gender fluid?

I don't care. I'm high and paranoid and lonely. It's as if a piece of shrapnel has slipped into me only I can't locate its point of entry because this creature is the baddest chick I've seen in the cramped bar with a greyhound circling a chintz lamp while people just keep drinking. Dee-light looks like a tall, dark-skinned Terence Trent D'Arby in dominatrix black heels, a fitted white dress with dangly bits like icicles falling; dark, androgynous, languid and seductive. An

American, her outfit encompasses not just her body but all the things it's transgressed, all the routes it's taken to get to the axis with me spinning on its tip. She takes a pull of her cigarette, cuts her eyes at me sideways, blows smoke out slowly. It's Berlin. It's Kreuzberg, 17 degrees Celsius out. I'm thawed from the cold but not my anxieties, not my demons. I want to roll them up and smoke them or somehow distil them in non-invasive ways but that hasn't been invented yet. There are bodies spilling from everywhere in the bar. It has two levels, is low-lit with a kind of shabby, industrial décor that's particular to Berlin. It should feel oppressive but doesn't. The Velvet Underground's album *The Velvet Underground & Nico* is playing. We're sitting on a worn, golden chaise longue, cushions at our backs, knees knocking against the small table of drinks.

I say, *My name's Kidd. I'm a musician.* She doesn't recognise it, doesn't know who I am. Fucking bliss.

What kind of music do you make?

Hip hop but not as you know it.

Well, anything can be not as you know it at any point.

Like Tricky.

I like Tricky.

The greyhound starts barking, having unwittingly developed a taste for alcohol through its orifices. Nobody seems to know who it belongs to.

Dee-light finishes off her cigarette, the smoke a breeze that's wrong-footed itself into another entity. She's speaking, her tongue curling in a liquorice mouth that's sweet tempting sour in a freefall.

Do you want to meet Herb? she asks.

Is that your friend?

No, baby, that's my penis, she coos, floating somewhere between the bar, the axis and Dante's Inferno.

My record company, ACR, let me have a two-month sabbatical after the last incident at a gig in Belarus where I howled on stage for half an hour, spilling my guts out onto the mic in a kind of personal exorcism. The audience thought it was part of the show. *Performance art meets hip hop!* one reviewer commented. Sinewy, macabre beats, stripped down to just my jeans and a red baseball cap, no lyrics because I'd forgotten. They'd departed my body, the country. They were trapped in my mouth, the border. At the time, I wondered what the audience made of me: a wiry, doe-eyed black man prowling the stage, eyes intermittently closed as if in prayer, the angle of spotlight falling on my sweat-covered body acting as a passageway, the giant screen capturing my movements. I howled an ancestor's cry that would mimic the lines of a body in the audience, like I'd spill goat's blood on the screen in an impromptu baptism of myself, like both ends of the stage had nurtured a quiet cacophony for the damned, which the mic hadn't picked up.

And so Berlin.

I like its slower pace. I like that I could cut a record here incognito and nobody would give a fuck. I could disappear in as much as a black man in Berlin can fly under the radar. I like some of the old memorial architecture, the Turkish areas, the cafés, the bakeries that pop up frequently. Every other person rides a bike. They have content expressions cycling through the city, their corner of a flattened atlas. I watch: it's a kind of meditation. I search for the scars of breaks just below the surface of skin. I contemplate the dichotomy of how black men really are and how the world expects us to be, how difficult it is to breathe between the tropes that come at you, the roles already written. I think of my own break before Berlin, tectonic plates shifting.

Really there was a series of incidents leading up to the storm. And you know a storm when it's coming. You let it take over your system because that's necessary in order for it to pass. It mutates in your veins. You become the antidote to your own virus.

I'm a lady you know, tra la la la la! Dee-light trills. *You're fucking handsome, you realise that?* she says, as we walk through an empty square. *You're surprisingly shy, a shy dude done good who wants to do bad things to me, tra la la la la!* She stops suddenly. She sticks her tongue out for me to suck and I do, hypnotised. It tastes of rum, brandy, sugar. It tastes like a clash of ingredients you shouldn't find in cocktails. We buy Früh Kölsch beers and ribs. We drink and eat at the apartment I'd been given inside a rambling building flanked by an art gallery. We talk for four hours straight.

We talk about *Invisible Man*, *Native Son*, about *The Black Jacobins* being an underrated work of genius, about Stuart Hall's ideologies, and nursing headaches listening to Sam Cooke.

Imagine what it's like to give birth in an inflatable garden pool, she says.

I don't know, I'm a man, I never think about those things.

I dreamed about it once. I'm Adam and Eve even though I don't believe in religion.

We argue over the last scene in *Carmen Jones*. I tell her Harry Belafonte is one of my heroes. She says, *I once audition for a production of* Carmen Jones *but they weren't ready, baby! My femme fatale Carmen would have brought an added dimension. The director kept trying to fuck me even though he had a wife.*

I say nothing to this, thinking she must get that all the time, straight men like me who find ourselves surprised by the things we want from her.

We hear a whimpering at the gate, then the sound of it being pushed. I look out of the window. The greyhound from the bar is poking its slender head through the gaps. Dee-light joins me, grabs a few bones from the ribs we'd eaten.

It could have anything, I warn.

So could you, baby, she retorts.

I watch her gently feeding it. It licks her hand gratefully afterwards before trotting away. Back inside, she takes her heels off again.

Doesn't it have an owner? I ask.

Strawberry? That dog followed me from Chicago. I used to see him eating out of the bins on the South Side.

It's ridiculous but I don't question it. She could have told me she was born under a magician's cape and I'd have offered her another spliff and gladly listened. I play Sun Ra on my laptop. When she starts gyrating slowly, talking about gateways in music, how we rebuild parts of ourselves there, I put the spliff down, get into bed to watch. *Shiiit.*

It's around 4 a.m. We're lying on the bed smelling of weed, alcohol, dipping our fingers into the curious parts of each other. We're so close it feels as though we're sharing the same breath.

Why do you call yourself Dee-light?

She strokes my head. *Close your eyes if you really want to know, baby.*

Everywhere we go people stare at Dee-light, six foot plus in heels, towering as if she's stepped off a billboard, a Ferris wheel or the place where bright entities can't be held down. People cluck like hens around us in curiosity.

Is she a model? Is that your girlfriend? Wow. I'm throwing

a party on a boat at the weekend, would she like to attend?
Nobody recognises me yet. Dee-light is her own celebrity,
effortlessly amassing a trail of fans wherever she goes. I'm
amused by the irony of this. I find it enchanting. I can live
vicariously through the elegant, sinewy lines of her body,
watch items get trapped in her walk; her fast mouth, quick
wit and humour are all hands from a deck of cards, with
Dee-light changing costumes in each card. We eat bland
ethnic food from places churning meals out for a broad
audience; mediocre Indian, tasteless Thai, disappointing
Taiwanese. It doesn't matter, Dee-light is feeding me in
ways I never planned for, like a curveball you have to catch
with both hands. Being with her is breathing again.

We walk around the city holding hands. I half expect the
greyhound to come crashing into us wielding a soiled playing card or part of the London skyline between its teeth.

At the Museum of Photography in Jebensstraße Dee-
light offers to read the receptionist's palm, an excitable,
mousy-haired, skinny woman who holds out her hands.

Dee-light runs her fingers over the woman's palms, starts
chanting in Xhosa.

Where are you from? the woman asks. *No, really, where
are you from?*

When people ask this, Dee-light's answer changes every
time. This time, though: *I'm from Mars, baby. Where
are you from?*

*

Two weeks pass. We're inseparable. Before I know it, Dee-light infiltrates my space; she is the curve of a kaleidoscope landed on a moon. I find her clothes in the closet: dark leather bustiers, candy-coloured giant platforms, lace panties of varying styles, mini dresses, a fake white fur coat *for when the occasion demands it, baby*, V-necked dresses, costumes, outfits from her burlesque days working at a club for liberated arbiters of immersive sensuality called Vedette on the outer edges of Bismarckstraße. There are four different-coloured wigs on eerily blank-eyed mannequins on the bathroom shelf. I picture them hurtling into unforeseen accidents, the wigs twitching on lampposts, street lights, road signs, over broken shards of glass from a rear-view mirror and Dee-light barefoot, clutching a handful of bones, crying out to a greyhound that'll come whenever she calls it. She buys spices from an African food festival, materials from Turkish flea markets, sweets from an Indian confectionery shop, an eggshell-coloured wedding cake because *Why should I wait to get married to eat good cake?* She listens to instrumentals on my laptop, leaves Post-it notes commenting on them around the flat: *Bravo! These beats feel Machiavellian* or *Go back in time and collaborate with George Clinton*. She cooks Hibachi soup singing OutKast's 'Prototype'. I start writing tracks. I'm excited by her, by the effect she has on me creatively. I sketch her in doorways on a small drawing pad I carry around.

I succumb to the infiltration. It's a relief, a space between languages. Its silences with items that don't belong to me yet become a part of my habitat. I circle them, stroke them, I give them room when necessary. They're physical elements and beyond them extensions of her, which find room in the spaces our bodies map.

I'm rummaging for eye drops one morning when I discover the pills in the spare bathroom cabinet. They look ordinary, harmless, tiny circles of white in small, off-yellow plastic containers. I study the labels, evidence that a transformation doesn't happen without some assistance. I hold one bottle. A light film of sweat covers my top lip. I roll the container in my hand, knowing the measurement of that one movement can't encapsulate the murkiness of digestible assistance. It settles in my head, a misshapen yellow fog that's its own season.

It's night time. We're sitting at both ends of the large kitchen window overlooking the city, smoking, the quiet hum of traffic playing in the background. Dee-light tells me she was once a chef at a place called the Ham & Hop in Chicago many moons ago. After that a flamenco dancer in Spain, after that part of a double drag act on a cruise line that ran from Anguilla to Santo Tomás, Guatemala. I watch her long throat; it doesn't look like a man's throat. It's regal. I see it stretching in the traffic, bending towards the movements of items from all its previous lives. Every movement is a way of seeing.

I wonder if each life just wasn't the right fit, or maybe they were. Maybe they were all meant to be temporary. Maybe the secret was to try to live them well, feverishly, because soon enough, they'd shrink in your grasp. I picture her outfits fraying in the blind spots of drivers, trying to communicate with a throat that could see. I blow smoke between her breasts. I imagine the dissatisfaction within her as a series of growing parched spots. I see the smoke winding its way in, losing my hands there as the result of a desire to have X-ray vision. I don't ask why Berlin for now. Berlin is initially a place of transition for people like Dee-light and me, but it has a magic that sucks you in. I don't tell her we met on the night of my arrival, that hours before I lay in the bedroom sweating and shaking so badly, I thought the crack in me had finally overwhelmed my body, that I felt I might die in an alien country, that I stumbled out into the darkness not knowing what to look for. But Berlin is the bastard of Bieniek and Newton: it can turn a personal catastrophe into a resurrection. And then I found Dee-light. It was like spotting a piece of stained glass on the train tracks, like discovering the right instrument to do yourself an injury with. I don't say any of this.

Instead I say, *The Ham and Hop, eh? So who was Ham and who was Hop?*

She doesn't answer. She stares into the evening lost in a memory, a grimace on her face, muttering, *Berlin.*

*

I wake up around 2 a.m. to hear Dee-light moving around the apartment restlessly. I'm caught in that space between sleep and growing alertness, the orbiting world outside now still around our indoor planet. The sounds seem muffled, as if sleep has been used as a cushion held over them. I hear what seems like the freezer being defrosted, the soft falling of ice, *whoosh whoosh*, the freezer drawers being pulled open, cutlery drawers yanked out, the hollows of pots and pans, picture Dee-light catching her reflection in the instruments of others. I'm rapidly discovering she has some strange habits, that those habits call to her at unexpected times. I pull the duvet back, slightly groggy, listen for the rhythm of her movements between the utensils. Just as I decide not to join her, I hear the spit and sizzle of oil in a pan. I sink back into the pillows. It's a fucking ungodly hour. Sometimes, you have to let a body work through the sharp utensils lodged in its radius.

In the morning, a contact signposts me to a studio in Pankstraße. I kiss Dee-light goodbye, head out into a balmy, bright day. I catch the U-Bahn from Schönleinstraße; the motions of the train feel comforting. It's a fairly full carriage. The gaunt-looking woman sitting beside me pulls out her make-up powder from a handbag bursting at the seams, dabs her nose, the bags beneath her eyes. I have the urge to get off at random stops to find surprise items on street corners, take them back to the apartment for Dee-light to rummage through whenever her hands become restless.

The studio is owned by a former music tour manager named Gunther, who's unable to keep still, has a penchant for Hawaiian shirts and a love of cognac. The studio's in a trailer tucked beneath railway arches. It feels oddly transient, like you could turn up one day and either the arches or the trailer would be gone. I spend a few hours laying down tracks, sharing cognac with Gunther in between, discussing the lost back catalogues of our favourite musicians gone too soon. I feel like myself again.

Other people trickle in and out. We become a ramshackle band of strays filling the trailer with random commentary and laughter.

Later, I return to the apartment to find the bedroom completely tossed, my laptop balancing precariously on the window sill and Dee-light naked in the corner. She's on a short pile of costumes, knees up, legs spread, taking sharp, short breaths as though trying to give birth. I grab her out of the birthing position. Her face is tear-streaked; eyeliner's smudged on her cheeks. *These hormones are making me crazy!* she yells, at the top of her voice.

I offer to pay for the full operation. *You know I can afford it. It's nothing, I'll get you to the best hospital*, I say, perched at the edge of the bed, opening my arms into the silence.

Fuck you. You don't know what it is to run from a name. She uncurls, drags out a pair of blue roller skates she'd stashed under the bed. She slips them on, glides into the kitchen, skating at full speed, launching herself at the corners of the room. As if those parts of the space are cuts with diamonds growing there, penis dangling, pubic hair a gnarly patch, barbed wire shrouding Mecca, breasts pert, dreads flying, dark skin like glazed molasses. I catch her when she skids. We collapse in the doorway. I wrap my arms around her with a growing sense of unease forming in my chest. Dee-light starts crying, the words coming thick and fast. As if they'd been waiting to spill out.

I loved the Ham and Hop. I was the best cook in the house. People used to say to me, Chester, I'll walk through brimstone to get to your grits and octopus soup. And I'd say, Don't hurt yourself, baby. Just come good, come correct opening hours, I'll serve you something worth the journey. And they used to come from all over Chicago for my jumbo pot, my lamb stew, my pecan pie, my surprise in the hen. Sometimes on weekends I'd work at the incinerator plant not too far away, but the Ham and Hop was my spot. The owner, Daryl, and I were lovers. Daryl was a church boy, charming as you please on the surface but with a mean streak that would convince Christ out of the notion of forgiveness. I never understood it. I loved him. I worked like a dog for him. He used to beat me so badly. Sometimes he'd fuck me, then beat me afterwards in a rage from nowhere. Hell, some nights I'd be serving customers with black eyes, limping taking orders, cooking with one broken arm. I used to dread waking up. Breathing hurt. I felt broken. I didn't know how I got to that place. All I did was love somebody, all I wanted was that love returned. Is that so bad? I just had enough.

Then one day, the police come by the restaurant. They say Daryl's missing two weeks, probably dead. They say there's blood all over his bedroom, bathroom. The attack was frenzied but they can't find no body. Without a body, they can't gather enough evidence, they can't prosecute. They say, Chester, hey, don't you work at the incinerator plant sometimes? Casually, like it ain't no thing. And you don't know anything?

Yes, sir, I say. I don't know anything. All I do is work in this here restaurant. I look 'em dead in the eye. I don't slip cos a black man caught slippin' is a dead motherfucker. They left with two slices of pecan pie. That week, I served three large pots of assorted meat and pumpkin soup. Customers loved it. They'd say, Goddamn, Chester, what's in this new soup you got on the menu? It's delicious. Can you give me the ingredients? I'm about to try this at home. I'd say, Naw, it's my grandmama's secret recipe.

Well, she did the rest of us a good service passing this on to you!

I'd just nod and smile. That's how I got through those days, nodding, smiling as if none of it was happening. It was Strawberry who saved my life. That damn dog turned up by the bins at the back of the Ham and Hop scavenging. He coughed Daryl's ring right into my hand. I knew it was Daryl's, see? It was gold with his first initial in black. Daryl was unimaginative like that. He used to pummel me in the ribs and head wearing that ring. I know it sounds crazy but Strawberry turned up on the cruise ships. He follows me wherever I go.

That's why I feed him when I can. I had to leave my name behind. I had to bury it. It was a sign that Strawberry brought the ring to me. I followed my instinct. I left Chicago. I got out, baby. I got out. Chester was dead. And Dee-light was there. Dee-light was always in me.

Her story leaves us both shaken. The air's been sucked out of the room. We're sylphs in a corner trying to feel our way in the dark, grabbing at fractured light from a combusted planet. I say, *I'm sorry, I'm so sorry.*

Don't be sorry, baby. Sometimes what we think are the right decisions take us the wrong way. That's not anybody's fault. It's just life.

The truth is, it's hard to know what to say that wouldn't somehow feel inadequate or trite or useless. What do you say to someone who got caught in an explosion?

I'm sorry you lost your legs. I'm sorry you may never walk again. There's a whole other life waiting for you on the other side. There is a series of small and large devastations to endure in order for you to get to it, in order for you to hold it with the limbs you do have left. I scan the room briefly; Dee-light's roller skates turn against the piles of chaos surrounding us. I get up slowly, remove my laptop from the window sill. Set it on the bed as though that one action will change the thoughts crossing each other, like tadpoles swimming upstream:

Dee-light's desire to give birth

A propensity for destruction

An ability to confide without admitting guilt

I take her to a Thai restaurant in the neighbourhood where there are large, red-paper lanterns dangling from the ceiling. The service is abrupt; the clock on the wall is permanently on 6 p.m. The stop in time feels like a blip, a loophole, a schism where we're shrunken, defenceless in the open tank, and the coiled black fish from an icy bottom are on tables ordering us instead. Later, we go to a club in Dorotheenstraße.

We take MDMA because we need to abandon ourselves temporarily. Everybody bleeds into each other. The frenetic beats are sirens calling, like an extinct tribe of birds in our veins. Dee-light attracts a crowd with her tribal, carnal-style dancing. I'm so gone, I don't pay too much attention to the male figure hovering beside me who fishes out a camera phone. The flash momentarily hurts my eyes, becomes a winged pale lens in my brain, ready to illuminate dormant memories I'd long buried.

I don't ask Dee-light how she got out of the States or if she must have missed the good things about home or what she did in order to survive those first few months of becoming a transient alien. I know I'll sketch her in exits that'll shape-shift, folding beneath the warmth of my breath. And she'll release the scarred limb she has hidden, letting it pierce through paper, concrete, cloud.

Her paranoia creeps in steadily. By the end of the first month, it's increasingly alarming. She continues to get up at odd hours, trudging through the apartment as though it's mountainous territory rather than flatland, as if the air at the top of the mountain's better. Her body on a loop, I find her repeatedly checking through the cupboards, the loft space, the wardrobe, under the bed, behind the doors. Blank-eyed, claiming, *Watchers are there, baby.* One time, on edge, she paces back and forth in the living room, finally looking at the street from behind gold curtains of the big window.

She tells me there's a man in a black Volkswagen Golf watching the apartment; he reads the *Chicago Tribune* at the wheel during breaks. I stand before the window in plain view. There are cars on either side of the boutique-lined street, a man at the top on the bench eating a *Quarkkuchen* from one of the Turkish bakeries, two people riding past on bikes, the cook from a steak house smoking outside it, strewn crackling leaves blowing to cover their eyes from the mutations of themselves in somebody else's vision. There is no man watching the apartment.

Another occasion, I find shaved pubic hair in the middle of the bed, gathered into a handful, a hairy nipple pro-truding from the sheets. I find a small plastic bottle of medication emptied into the toilet, floating, waiting to transform into a white hovercraft or a small gateway in the toilet's neck.

I think of Ferris wheels, planes, helicopters. It doesn't matter what mode of transport you take to get high, the drop is always sudden when it comes.

She hides my passport. *You know the watchers will use it against us. Those motherfuckers are creative, baby! I'm protecting you. I wouldn't put anything past them.*

The record company calls. The photo of Dee-light and me at the club has surfaced on blogs, gaining traction. It's joyous. We're dancing under twisting lights. My eyes are bright. It's the other side of a coin, a kind of happiness, similar to when Dee-light read me pages from Alexander Dumas's *The Three Musketeers*, commenting that people in conflict with themselves should anchor their bodies in metaphysical ways.

The record label releases a story that Dee-light is my distant cousin. They take control of the narrative before it becomes a story. They spin until she's relegated to the sidelines, then erased. I try to imagine us just being in London. I can't. A place for misfits, Berlin is our bubble, our safety net. In London, my family and friends would never understand somebody like Dee-light or why I'm drawn to her.

I become ashamed of the fearful feeling blooming inside me. It's a razor's edge sprouting underneath my tongue.

*

I find my passport at the back of the wardrobe. I don't say a word, slipping it into the hidden compartment of my luggage. Our evenings become a crumbling bank where paranoia and uncertainty fester. I watch her constantly. It's exhausting.

One night for relief, I head over to Gunther's to record some more tracks. We have a meal out afterwards. He gifts me a Hawaiian shirt as a memento. I'm touched by this.

On my way back, Berlin feels magical again. It's a luminous night: the sky's dappled with half thoughts that become stars; the squares are empty except for the odd pigeon feeding on leftovers of earlier scenes. There's a chill in the air; condensation on shop windows waters my reflection, encouraging it to slip on Gunther's gift as we both walk through the city trying to gather ourselves, one on concrete, one through glass.

At the apartment, I discover Dee-light in the kitchen on the floor, surrounded by pots, pans, cutlery. Strawberry circles the display of chaos, his damp footprints drying. Dee-light is rocking something wrapped up in a small, pink blanket, cooing at it.

Light from the lamp on the table feels insufficient as a slow horror spreads from my stomach right up to my throat. I flick the light switch on the wall to check the scene before me isn't a trick that came through the window. I take tentative steps forward. There's a screaming in my head now, a splintering of sounds in my ears, an acknowledgement that this is the line, this is the point at which things change. To behave otherwise would be akin to a naked man heading into a blizzard, a diver without an oxygen tank, a woman looking for water in a gutted well only to remember she's fifty per cent liquid. The rush of blood to my head is so intense, it's an effort to stand up. It's an alarm acknowledging my lover holding a stolen pale baby up to me just as it lets out a high-pitched squeal, curling its fist. And my wild-eyed lover says, *This is our son, baby. Isn't he cute?*

At that moment, it feels absolutely urgent to ask. It feels necessary. I can't believe I didn't before. *Did you kill Daryl?*

Strawberry emerges from under the table, licking the right side of Dee-light's face. The pots try to carry the short silence, the gulf expanding.

Bearing the most innocent expression, Dee-light answers, *Well, Strawberry killed him each time.* As if Daryl had been killed more than once.

Dee-light informs me she stole the baby from a hospital. I'm fucking astonished that a five-foot-eleven black trans woman was able to walk away from a Berlin hospital with somebody else's baby but Dee-light is a ventriloquist, even on the edge, able to disappear through the hospital's blind spots, like an audacious magician's apprentice.

We dress up as drag queens. I wear a silver wig, paint my lips metallic grey. We find a Nissan Primera, hot-wire it. Dee-light reluctantly puts the baby in the back.

The drive to the hospital is tense. My nerves are shredded, the baby's screaming. Dee-light becomes hysterical, pummelling me on the side of my face. I try to steer the vehicle on course, one hand on the wheel. It swerves from side to side as I fight Dee-light off with the other hand. My foot on the gas sporadically freezes, as though it'll become a sketch I drew, a slice of wedding cake, a piece of evidence from a crime scene.

At the hospital, I leave Dee-light in the car. I drop the baby off on the reception desk when the attendant heads out for a toilet break. I look down the polished corridors, shiny gauntlets in the night. I scan the immediate vicinity for cameras but can't spot any. We gently pull away from the hospital car park. Dee-light is silent.

Her previous words echo inside a car that belongs to neither of us.

A black man caught slippin' is a dead motherfucker.

Sweating profusely, I exert more pressure on the gas. I snatch the silver wig off, throw it into the back seat where it takes root in a newborn's distant cry.

At the apartment, Strawberry's footprints have vanished from the kitchen floor. I crush sleeping pills in a glass of Amaretto, hand it to Dee-light, *To help you relax*, I say.

When she stumbles around in the bedroom, clutching at me feebly, there's a pained expression on her face; the realisation at the depth of my betrayal crumpling her features before she collapses on the bed, it's the action of a whirlpool soaking into a mattress.

I pack. I leave nothing. I abandon Dee-light in the apartment out cold on the bed. I cry silently at my cowardice. I exit the bubble that's become warped in our clutches. I catch a night flight back to the UK. I tell myself this is what must be done.

A year passes. My record is number three in the charts. I'm at Gatwick airport. I hear it playing on the radio in the duty-free shop. It feels like a hammer's been thrown through my chest, a horizon dislodged from there I can never get back. I buy the largest bottle of Opium perfume from the shop, knowing it'll be taken from me. But it's Dee-light's favourite. I spray it on my hand, sniffing like a starved man. I'm en route to Reykjavik for a show. I'm fucking bone tired. The kind of tired that would make you sleep only to forget yourself when you wake up, the perfect opening for a reinvention. On the plane, I turn the perfume lid over in my fingers, like a small planet. The plane takes off, rises steadily. Everything becomes a model version of itself, fading away. I think of Dee-light, of muted light falling on her skin in bars. I think of her head turning on the creases in pillows, of infernos on cold streets becoming pathways. I think of her liquorice mouth, a bud in me constantly reassembling. I think of glass rims and dogs that belong to no one being springboards, of fans who don't know my album, *Inertia*, was inspired by a trans woman who roller skates naked indoors, who, like a goddess, tethers on the edges of a landed comet.

Love is a kind of madness.

I think of Berlin. I think of Dee-light.

I can't extrapolate one from the other.

Addendum

After the bone on the mountain top
After the crawl in the midnight field
After the dog costumes barking in white water
After the tinfoil creatures with sullied mouths
After a reckoning on the bruised margin
You want to build a raft
You hold the core of me with a burning hand
And press your bloodshot eye to the fold.

Cornutopia

My pain weighed eight and a half stone. Imagine dragging eight and a half stone of extra shit around? That's an entire person. That's tonnes of chocolate to exist on for at least two months if you're resourceful. That's a small person and possibly a baby in a Halloween costume together. Anyway, I did what the booklet said, you know? I stood naked in the mirror wearing that red hard hat with the wires poking from it that reminded me of those joke beer hats you get at Christmas, which have multiple plastic tubes sticking out, like translucent Medusa snakes. The little numbers screen on it sped up as it calculated. I felt a rush of anticipation when that happened, because who would ever imagine you could quantify combined hurt, which is what pain is? Combined hurt accumulated over time, which left you aching, rolling, gnawing and howling at your own image. All the hurts some-how galvanised into tiny foot soldiers treading the injuries inside you. I lifted my arms in the mirror while the hat calculated, like I'd hover off the carpet and hurtle into my own reflection, as though it was an imposter. I'd taken off my socks, my silver wind-chime-shaped earrings, the green bracelet I'd bought from a flea market at Brick Lane because the weathered-faced woman selling them had a small knob at the edge of her fifth finger, like a sixth finger that had stubbornly refused to grow. Afterwards, I opened the bedroom window, knocking the small cactus on the cracked white ledge, bits of soil spilling, a waft of cold air tingling my skin. The sounds of tyres, traffic and footsteps in the snow were a cold slush rapidly melting in my eardrums. The cavern inside me unfurled, flickering. Hoof-tipped creatures limped out from the quiet chasm breathing, bending their limbs, vying for the hat. I tugged it tighter, felt a light prick just above my ear, then a trickle of blood slithering, landing on a hoof trapped in the mirror, staining the sixth finger growing in the window-ledge crack. Light-headed, I rushed to the mirror again. A volt of electricity was looking for its reflection. The hoof pulsed in the glass from the weather in my room.

I watched a light drizzle of snow falling for a few moments, steadying my breathing, hands on the window sill, in the spilled soil brushing the foreign growing sixth finger communicating silently with the hoof. I remembered that I used to have a recurring dream about ventriloquist dolls tumbling in the air through angles of snow, as though being baptised, the sly white tufts melting into their sinister expressions. And each time they landed, they searched for

different things: pink tongues curled into the white, boomerangs they'd use for their next stretch of flight, damaged
hearts, which were bombs ticking in the snow, waiting to
explode at the feet of children threading between pavements, in the gazes of foxes at night, rummaging through
overgrown shrubs, in the blind spots of bruised women
wandering the city. Once I woke up embracing some of
the items the dolls had gathered, my fingertips lost in their
edges, fingers numbed from the cold, my body drenched in
sweat, stomach convulsing in pain, chest a concave tunnel
the dolls' footsteps rang loudly in. I almost fell off the bed,
the white sheet tangled at the bottom between my legs, the
items vanishing in the charged night air, damp outlines on
the bed waiting to slip onto other surfaces. I'd stumbled
from the bed, out of a cold embrace, the glass of water on
the side dresser spilling, the glass rolling in the same ham-
pered movement, the stars threatening to break through
the marked ceiling, its pattern of shell shapes undulating
slowly, disorienting me. I lifted the tumbler, standing it up
on the dresser emptied. I tripped over the duvet on the
floor, a cotton sea of misshapen planes and angles. The cold
air dimpled my skin. I shivered. The open window flapped
back almost rebelliously. I stuck my head out of it for a few
minutes to allow the rush of cool air to reset it. After closing it, I perched at the edge of the bed, listening for items
shaken from snow to thwack against the glass.

*

I called Edwin. What better way to temper any ridiculous overexcitement? He picked up after four rings. I heard a crackle, a rising of sound, like something in the frequency had expanded, sliding through the wires into points of electricity the immediate eye couldn't see. In the past, when such occurrences happened, we'd exacerbate each other's paranoia.

They're watching us, Edwin would say. *I'm telling you, this fucking government is increasingly invading our lives. They've done it with CCTV already. How many of those things do I need crawling up my arse? I can't scratch my balls without seeing one. It's big business, just like the prison system in America making money out of caging black bodies, capitalist bastards.*

I'd cradle the receiver, feeling its heat against my neck, braids tousled by my fingers, the phone's battery indicator, a tiny bubble of red light, flashing in my peripheral vision, its buttons pressing into my face. *What if they start putting things in the food if they're not doing it already? You know how fizzy drinks make kids crazy!*

I'd pad about the flat talking animatedly to him about anything and everything because that was us. That was Edwin, my ally, my kemosabe, my ex-boyfriend and prior to that my ex-fuck-buddy. Edwin, who'd given me the best head of my life, who'd never judged my sexual proclivities instead commenting during one past tryst, *How many tricks you got, girl? You just put the* Kama Sutra *out of business!*

Oh ... shit. Do that again. You'll make a black man lose his sight. You know we need to see in this world.

Edwin was a location scout for a film production company. All six foot two of him was rangy, bearing a languid power that could surprise you with its intensity. He was bright-eyed, dimple-cheeked, bespectacled, attractive. Intellectual. He could quote Proust and Garvey in one turn of phrase, but if you underestimated him, if you fucked with him in the wrong way, he'd show you how a Hackney boy rolled (Hackney before hipsterism, that is). At university, he'd got a first in political science and loved the arts. He liked his brogues dark, thought Lupita Nyong'o was better-looking than Beyoncé, had a mighty crush on Sade, preferred full-proof rum to my palm wine, was on the board of his local arts hub, the Bernie Grant Centre. When he got irritated, his eyes would narrow, his gaze zeroing in on you as though he had X-ray vision. He never forgot my birthday and would send me a postcard from wherever he travelled to without fail.

Hey, I said, into the crackly void. *Where are you? I'm anxious, I weighed it.*

Ladybird. He chuckled. His nickname for me since our first meeting at a hot-dog stand at Womad Festival where I'd run out of cash to pay. He'd stepped in, then casually suggested we catch a few bands together.

I'm not offended by those ugly wellingtons by the way. I

just like the way you rock them, he'd commented, referring to the bright purple sunflower-splashed boots I'd bought last minute.

I'm equally not offended by that hideous Hugh Masekela T-shirt because at least you have good taste in music, I'd retorted. We'd laughed, wolfing down our hot dogs afterwards. He waxed lyrical about cosmic expansion, the sun beating down on the paths we wove through tents, stands, shuddering music stages. Edwin's low-timbred voice had been like a liquid concoction my limbs were drawn to, our shadows rustling in tepee tents for seeds suffering from heatstroke while we wandered.

I tugged the dark phone cord around a finger, releasing a slow breath.

In the kitchen, cooking a chicken bird, Edwin continued. *The whole people volunteering for medical studies is a weird thing to me but I support you using your agency.*

I heard his background noise of cupboards being flung open, the fridge groaning, rummaging, a burst of tap water in the sink. I pictured him in the Popeye apron I'd bought him, loosely tied, smiling internally. Those elegant, tapered hands I knew gutting, weighing, cutting, holding a cluster of tiny yolks between his fingers, squeezing until it spilled its yellowy confession of lost birth on the metallic sink. Edwin moved between the onyx-coloured counter tops, his main audience a surreal poster of Josephine Baker above the fridge, while the fans she held turned slowly, maybe Miles Davis's *Bitches Brew* spinning on the record player.

Are you sure you want this? he asked. *If it's the money, I can loan you some. Pay me back whenever you can. No problem.*

It's not the money, I said, a little irritated. *I need to try something else. It's hard sometimes.* My voice sounded high, defensive. *What are you doing now?* The jangle of cutlery rang through.

Chopping. Listen, I want you to call me if anything—

I will. I clicked off, still seeing him in his kitchen, feeling breath breaking limb, yolk floating inside chest, my naked body on a chopping board covered with chicken skin. And Edwin holding a knife, poised to debone me if I asked.

A tension crept into my back, something that always happened when I felt the panic in me rising. Soon the pain would come, forcing me to practise breathing techniques, stretches in the centre of the room, like an acrobat with limited potential pulled out of a box, dusted down, prodded not to perform for audiences but to navigate the traumas of life, which disguised themselves wrapped in silk material, charming seemingly harmless people, yet always possessed a molten core, a runny soft centre of opaque liquid that could destroy you. My left foot went numb from pins and needles. A pain split the inside of my head, like the edge of a guillotine. Suddenly the room was a reflection escaped from a trick mirror. The picture on the orange wall of four naked black women standing on a riverbank holding scarves shaped like bird heads trembled. The women turned around, made a space for me to join them, followed by our leap into the water, the bird heads flattening around us. An old chest of drawers with my underwear and socks peeking out became tongues wagging, waiting to take flight. The stash of sixties doo-wop records in a tray by the handful of incense sticks broke through their sleeves in revolt at confinement; the incense sticks in weathered shelves had tips that glowed amber, calling to a stray strand of smoke that was making its way into the fray. Books on the table, including Ralph Ellison's *Invisible Man*, Amos Tutuola's *The Palm-Wine Drinkard*, Jacqueline Woodson's *Brown Girl Dreaming*, were open to thumbed corners, underlined passages, paragraphs that had been indented in my mind for kernels of knowledge, grains of comfort, ways to reconstruct myself. I half expected to reach for the wardrobe doors, opening them to find items for survival instead of clothes: an oxygen mask, a small inflatable raft, a compact defibrillator. The pain intensified. The flash of a blade was cutting through the chaos, a ripple of blood on it to revive the bird heads in the photograph. My pain became keloids on a high wire waiting for me to claim them one by one. Almost blindingly, I reached for the *Cornutopia* booklet on the bed, an exotic butterfly coughed up from a bed sheet.

Our drug trials help push the boundaries of medicine, the strap line read. I imagined anything that could help, provide some relief. I placed a finger on the octagon-shaped logo at the top right corner of the page as though it was a beating heart. The red hat rattled with the contents of my head. The string of keloids fell down from the high wire; I the acrobat dodged them before they found new entry points in my skin. The hoof from the mirror broke through, bearing shards of glass, cantering frenetically to the sound of a distant rubble approaching. I looked in the mirror. The room balanced dangerously on the splayed booklet, buoyed by the possibility of light.

I packed enough for one week, the length of time the trial would last. At the ashy grey building in Camberwell, near the old Maudsley Hospital, I followed the sign for the trials area, a green arrow with the words *Drugs Trials This Way*, the black font leaning slightly to the right as if bracing itself for keen hands, breath, wear and tear, slowly edging away until it departed the white space. I crossed a series of passageways. The floors gleamed. Uniformed bodies milled about; the odd cash and vending machines popped up, barely any sandwiches in them, plus all the shit chocolate bars you didn't want to eat, crisps you wouldn't swallow unless the food on offer was absolutely diabolical, which was usually the case. Hospitals seemed always to offer the runt of everything. *A new anti-depressant that could take the pain away.*

That's what the *Cornutopia* brochure said. Still in the

early stages, a drug that could revolutionise the market, much like Prozac did in the early eighties. I wondered if they'd tested it on animals yet. Did they test anti-depressants on animals? I wasn't even sure. The volunteers were the guinea pigs. The ruined batch, our innards on Petri dishes to be studied, dissected, moulded. I wasn't the first to have wandered through hospital doors unsure of what lay ahead. A gaunt orderly wheeling blood samples nodded at me, his greying moustache patchy. The clinky motion of small tubes of blood was oddly comforting. I imagined him having an accident up ahead, the tubes fall-ing to the floor shattering, snakes of blood released from their confines, splattering onto his dulled, pale blue scrubs.

The Weisler building where the trials were being held was somewhat removed from the rest of the hospital, as if it was likely to cross into another dimension, the wards spilling pills from its cracks, stethoscopes scouring for the faint lines of illnesses in chests expanding in the wind. I walked through metallic double doors, tugging the large aqua-coloured cloth bag of belongings on my shoulder.

Good morning! A nurse clutching a sick bowl beamed.

Welcome, we hope you have a good experience here, another offered brightly, as if I was a passenger on a flight to Zanzibar and she a flight attendant.

I walked over to the reception area to sign in. Texted Edwin.

The staff here are really happy. It's weird. This is a twi-light zone.

The receptionist typed on her keyboard, smiling, pulling up my details on the screen, discreetly glancing at the scarred ring of skin on my throat.

I touched the scar, my fingers trembling against the circumference of it, a tattoo made with a knife.

Edwin and I had been dating for roughly a year on that wintry night. We'd just had dinner at an Ethiopian restaurant in London Bridge. Edwin needed to fly out first thing for a location hunt in Malta so we parted ways at a set of traffic lights before the bus stop I needed to catch a bus home, kisses lingering, hands reluctant to let go, soft laughter bubbling out. For some reason, rather than catch a bus as planned, I decided to take the subway towards the station instead. A split-second decision I'd agonise over in months to come. But I was buoyant, intoxicated from the pleasure of spending time with a man who seemed to adore me. I entered the low-lit passageway taking cold air into my lungs, heels clicking on the ground, black gold-trimmed vintage bag swaying against my pleated skirt, trying to lull a crease into submission. A man appeared on the opposite side, as though released from a puppeteer's hand; bulky, dark-haired, bearded. I half smiled then looked away. Before I knew it, he was at my side asking for the time. Panicked at his closeness, the narrowing of his weasel-like brown eyes, his speed despite the breadth of him, the immediate chill that sank into my bones, as if a temperature dial had been turned down inside me, I flicked my wrist up, feigning calmness. *Sure*, I said. *It's eleven thirty p.m.*

Something shifted, a flash of fury appeared in his eyes. He punched me in the face.

The force of it was so sudden, so jarring, I thought the impact would knock my head off clean, send it spinning into the air. Stunned, I stepped back lifting my hands up defensively, tasting blood running from my nostrils.

Oh, God, take the money. Take my handbag, I offered, shaking uncontrollably, my heartbeat pounding, galloping to meet the man's fists to plead on my behalf.

Don't fucking speak, you bitch! he ordered tersely, dragging me to the side, forcing me down, his eyes glassy as though the shadows of cruelties were waiting to break through the irises. I cowered on the ground. He kicked my trembling, hyper-alert body repeatedly, stomping on my head till I felt it would crack, like a soft shell beneath the complicit light's gaze. Pain shot from my head to the very core of me.

I knew I would never forget his black windbreaker with its checked collar, the smell of cheap aftershave on his skin, a faint scent of tobacco on his breath, dried piss on the wall, his ink-stained large hands, as if he'd been handling a leaky pen hours before. The pen's ink was spent. Its cracked, slim body lay in the puppeteer's hand.

Every element would remain emblazoned in my memory. Just when I thought I couldn't take any more pain, he knelt astride me, pinning me down. Defiantly, I started fighting then, gathering every ounce of energy I could from the centre of me, which had moved from a force so great it was pressed against my ribs.

I struggled beneath him, kicking in a newly invented stroke. The weight of him was too much, the heat off his skin, his sweaty mass, his sheer desire to destroy was an impossible molten bridge to cross. I saw the flash of the blade from the corner of my eye, my head was yanked back. I couldn't scream, my voice was mangled to a whisper, panicked. I felt the blade on my throat, a slitting, a quick motion to the right, a mercy of sorts indicating the ordeal was nearly over, followed by an unbearable pain, blood spilling, my head snapping in a forward motion.

A weight lifted as he got off me, my heartbeat cantering back into my chest from a failed excursion beyond its wall of muscle. I lay on the harsh, cold ground gurgling, woozy, seeing the blood from my throat form an impromptu map with runny outlines. Everything became faint. And the irony of Edwin, long gone in the opposite direction, didn't escape me, listening to the funk playlist I'd made him while I fought for my life.

A chilly night. A vicious, random attack. No items stolen; no bank cards, no credit cards, no cash, no jewellery taken, just an unexplained encounter with a stranger that would leave an indelible, alien fingerprint on my life. Just my limbs going into shock in that tunnel as I desperately clung to the edges of everything I thought I knew while the footsteps of somebody running to save me took on an almost mystical quality in the days to come, as did other elements: the ambulance siren breaking through the fog, like a startled seraph, my body being lifted, a rush of voices speaking in urgent tones, a thinning, warped musical note, the squeaky wheels of the ambulance bed interrupting, the cold hand inside me hovering over my heartbeat, turning into clay, the night's traffic zipping past a tentacled tragedy.

And later, the scar on my throat a constant reminder, a permanent necklace of taut, shinier skin, a certificate of near death I wore on my body.

Months after it happened, I went over everything with a fine-tooth comb, weighed up every possible past misdeed I'd done to warrant such a comeuppance.

Perhaps I'd been mean to my attacker's sister at school and forgotten. But I was never a bully. I despised them. I was always the kid or teenager who befriended outsiders because they felt like my tribe, kin stitched together from the feeling of difference, being in between or just outside. Perhaps I'd been rude to him at a club years back during my early twenties when I'd shot my mouth off at young men invading my personal space too eagerly, drink in hand. There had been no inkling of familiarity, no recognition. And I was good with faces. I rarely forgot one once I'd interacted with somebody, even on the smallest level.

Perhaps he'd been hovering menacingly in the background while Edwin and I chatted on the walk back from the restaurant. That couldn't have been the case.

Edwin would have spotted him. He'd have insisted on escorting me halfway through my journey if not all the way. Perhaps he just didn't like the look of me in that subway, the way I walked, the way I'd angled my head curiously before blinking, looking away, before the moment he struck. Perhaps he'd wanted to cut me down to size, fell me as if I were a moving tree. There was no explanation.

He was never caught.

When there is no reason, you become obsessed with finding answers. Every possibility was an answer shot with morphine before fading away. And Edwin cutting his trip short to fly back to be by my bedside after the attack, a terrible silence between us, the weight of his collapsed, forlorn expression disintegrating, the quiet panic in his bloodshot eyes. His anger at himself for what he saw as his failure to protect me was palpable, emanating from every coiled movement. His shoulders crumbled because he knew.

He knew nothing would ever be the same again.

By 11 a.m. there were at least thirty trial participants in adjoining wards, perched on the beds in pale hospital gowns after restlessly claiming their individual spaces, rummaging through bags, peeking in the empty cupboard spaces beside the pillow end, moving the curtains, testing the beds, smiling distant nervous smiles at each other. A whiteboard with our names written in red felt by the doors overlooked our hive-like activities. The doctors and a few nurses arrived, white uniforms starched to perfection, their manner warm, encouraging, their faces masks of congeniality. I'd never seen such positive medical staff. Everything was 'wonderful' and they were 'so pleased' to have us participate in the study. We were given medication in tiny plastic containers, two pills shaped like small capsules, the top half white, the bottom purple. After they left, I grabbed my set of playing cards from the inside back pocket of my bag, sat cross-legged on the bed laying them out, as if I'd unearth something inside them while the clock hands on the wall ticked in a content silence.

Around 2 p.m. I felt light, happy, the ache inside me dulled. I noticed the other participants were wandering around listlessly, their pupils dilated, expressions of euphoria on their faces. I got off the bed feeling higher and higher, as if balancing on a tightrope stretched across two skyscrapers. Bright purple mushrooms sprang from the floor, their bulbous heads dampening against my feet; small, speckled dawns grew in the sick pans. The ward seemed tropical, warm. The walls became silvery waterfalls; our names on the whiteboard were red gateways to put our fists through. I noticed newborn black babies bearing circular scars on their throats crawling under the beds, spitting playing cards from their mouths. Curtains of slanted light fell from the ceiling. I reached into them, grabbing knife edges turning into keys. People hugged, laughed breathlessly, ran their fingers over each other's skin as though it was new terrain to discover, pressed their ears against pulse points threatening to break the skin, wanting to capture every essence of being alive. They stuck keen tongues out to catch the elixir falling through the roof. It was almost childlike. My pain had waned.

This. This was the plane I wanted to be on. My pain was reduced to a molecule, a glimmer under a telescope, a tiny tremor in a riverbank. I fished my mobile phone out. It had three bars left. I texted Edwin. *I feel amazing! Can you tell from where you are? Can you feel it?!!*

Ah, I'm glad, Ladybird, stay up. Xx

Nurses came before they faded away. They left jugs of water we consumed rapidly, trickles running down the sides of our mouths. I was vaguely aware of a few nurses hovering on the periphery, breaking through the lines to leave bruised pears, bananas, apples, teeth-marks in fruit and the teeth-marks abandoning the fruit in search of other skin to mar. The doctors appeared again too, scribbling notes while peering at us curiously, fixed smiles on their faces, watches glinting in their pockets. They seemed unfazed by the contained chaos, making no efforts to order us to behave, as if we were unruly children. They turned their backs, figures vanishing through the swinging doors after jotting down odd equations on the whiteboard beside our names, which fractured into red gate-ways. I walked towards the doors, the showers of light warm on my skin. I felt feverish, intoxicated. The mushrooms beneath my feet were bending and swaying with every step I took. I exited the doors, turned left, passing the messy stash of files on the empty reception desk. I headed to the next ward. By now half of my body had sprouted new growth: rose-coloured seashells with the sound of shores beneath them, autumnal leaves crackling, dragonfly wings flapping at a rapid speed that would be impossible to measure. I stood outside the ward watching through the glass. Some bodies were splayed on the floor, arms outstretched. A man whose robe had come undone had his tongue pressed against a trolley wheel, eyes closed in bliss; by the window a flush-faced, pudgy woman was rocking a folded green jumpsuit in her arms as though it was a child and cooing at it. One man lay in bed holding a broomstick, having a conversation with it. Another woman was crawling on the floor, gathering the movements of shapes that mutated against her fingers. A nurse breezed past me, smiling without a care in the world, whistling. My head began to throb. Everything was a joyous assault on the senses, a riot of colour, a combustion of drunken atoms. I pushed back against the door, against the weight of it, opening it, letting the things that had grown on my body flutter in, fragmenting in different directions. My dragon-winged cries met the lines of stunted shores.

*

I crashed out, levelled off. I woke up in a laundry cupboard spun at an angle, clinging to a bottle of Comfort fabric softener as though my life depended on it. I was surrounded by the artificially constructed smell of meadows on bed sheets I panicked would flutter up to suffocate me, like a scene from any of the *Final Destination* movies where death was inescapable, no matter how obscure, how slim or remote the chances of certain elements converging to result in my unfortunate demise. I had cramps in my stomach. I swung my legs out before gently leaping off the large bottom shelf space I couldn't remember crawling into. Tiny shafts of light filtered through the grooves at the base of the door. I pressed my fingers against those grooves, as though trying to reclaim my prints, and evidence of a moving, bright Mecca that had waned in my misguided quest to find it even more limbs. I stumbled out onto the hallway, a winding corridor with passing figures of hospital staff changing gears in the evening. I arrived back at the ward to find Eden had gone, its fruit dissipated to points in the air that flickered tauntingly, briefly. The other trial participants were meek and mumbling in their beds, tiny doors within them creaking, the hinges medicated, loosening, tremors from their hearts temporarily dormant having got lost in the traffic of molecules shifting, in the electric buzz of brains rewiring.

By late evening an erratic, sallow-skinned, auburn-haired attendant wielding a benign grin and a trolley full of fruit salad, hardened roast chicken, potatoes and the next round of medication arrived. This time we were given two blue capsules each. I skipped the chicken, which could have doubled as a weapon to bludgeon someone with, picked at the potatoes and softened fruit salad due to my cramps.

Late at night, I heard a siren from every corner of the ward: damaged, misshapen bloody hearts were beating in the sick pans. The walls were shedding their layers to reveal scar tissue. Drip bags on silver stands had pulses morphing into fungal-like slugs, slowly changing the liquid to the hues of a traffic light. The ceiling rattled. I saw myself crawling along the window pane, around the edges of the ward to peek into the mouths of the other trial participants, dark caverns containing the strap of a blood-smeared, vintage handbag I'd misplaced there. Clammy and short of breath, I checked my phone. Two bars left. I texted Edwin.

This is fucking terrifying.

He responded. *Want me to come get you? Xx*

I switched the phone off.

I sat up in bed scratching my scar for at least ten minutes.

Four days into the study and I was a wreck. My hands shook often. My anxiety and paranoia were even more exacerbated by the surroundings. I struggled with insomnia and strange visions in the day. The pain had slunk back, burning with the ardour of wandering embers that found their way into areas of excavation inside me. I'd lost my appetite, which wasn't helping. I was shrinking. The hospital gown was baggy, askew on my thinning frame. My eyes were hollowed chambers, my stomach cramps unpredictably assailing me at the most inopportune moments.

Late one afternoon, I cornered a nurse by the whiteboard in my ward, a fidgety woman wearing oddly elaborate Dame Edna-style glasses. Her fox-like face was overly made-up, make-up slathered on as if to hide something. Her brow furrowed at my approach.

I'm not reacting well to the meds. The levels are all wrong! Shouldn't I be feeling better? I want to leave, I said, adjusting the sleeves of my gown, feeling like one giant tic, like a recurring spasm. I scratched a scab on the inside of my left wrist.

She waited a few seconds. The corners of her mouth curved upwards, wine-red lipstick somewhat faded on her thin lips. *Everybody's different. It takes a little while for people's systems to adjust to the levels. You've been here two weeks already. You signed up for a month. All you need is a nice cup of tea.*

You can't leave. She grabbed my elbow, firmly steering me back towards the beds. She'd batted away my concern like a pro.

It had appeared again, that polite detachment, false warmth from the staff, which was increasingly making me uneasy. Two weeks had gone quickly. Had I really signed up for a month? I couldn't remember. I sat up in my bed waiting, picking at my wrist scab, listening to the idle chatter of other participants, the gentle sway of the open window and what sounded like a car screeching to a halt in the distance. Once I spotted the desk opposite the three wards was empty of staff on a late lunch, I sprang into action, sluggish but still fairly mobile. I headed for the desk. Not knowing what exactly I was looking for, I sifted through stashes of X-rays, green prescription slips, notes, pills in sealable plastic bags. Underneath one bag, I found the key for the grey cabinet behind the desk. It was attached to a small sloth key-ring. After checking for passers-by, I opened the cabinet, my fingers running over the project Cornutopia patient files. I opened a few individual ones, recognising some of the participants. My fingers went further back, plucking more files, as if from a reachable dark ether. I opened those too. I recognised some of the staff.

A chill hit me, flooded my bones. There was a jangling in my nerves that sounded like a thousand tiny chimes suffused in my blood.

The staff on the wing were former patients. God only knew what had been done to the original team running the trial. I thought of the orderlies wheeling food in, the nurses and doctors I'd encountered, how their benign smiles had seemed so placid, harmless. I sensed an alarm moving in, ready to shatter over the files. I put everything back including the key. My body shook as I made my return to my bed.

I grabbed my mobile, stashing it in the gown's pocket, then headed to the disabled toilet further along the corridor. Only a vending machine quietly murmuring was a witness, waiting for the drop of items, the echo of something lost that came with each one.

The sensation I felt was not like having the ground pulled from under you, more like falling down an endless chute sucking your most present memories away. My heart rate sped up. Inside the toilet I switched the phone on. Only one bar left, flicking, its power ebbing away. I called Edwin, and struggled to talk as the scarred walls closed in.

I was weak, spent, the pain spreading from my centre. He picked up, listening to my rush of garbled panicked breaths that sounded like a kind of static.

Edwin and I sat on the bench in the park nearby, watching the ducks flapping frantically at each other, bumbling past, taking off to a horizon that had wept earlier in the day. My hospital gown fluttered against my thigh. The scab on my wrist was now fully picked off, the skin underneath raw. The name tag on my wrist jutted against Edwin's grey coat sleeve in a convenient alliance; the tag read *Amel Dyani*. I glanced at my name again briefly, distantly, as though it belonged to someone else. I was exhausted. I leaned against Edwin. He kissed my forehead tenderly. The pain was oozing out of me, clotted and slimy, slippery. It slithered over the grass, the circular strip of concrete, the daisies twitching. It slid up the trunks of trees, clung to their leaves like dew. People were skidding on my pain. I felt weaker and weaker, the hum in my brain becoming smaller, reduced to a dot of sound. I stared at the pain stretched before me, a film of cellophane, marvelling at its hue, its density, its pliability. It just kept crawling, crawling, crawling towards other openings. Edwin grabbed my hand. I raised my head. *I did the right thing, didn't I?* I muttered feebly, cracked lips stinging.

Yeah, Ladybird, he said, looking me dead in the eye. *Veni, vidi, vici.*

A tear ran down his cheek. The cold air was biting and of little comfort. A toy rocket whizzed past, landing in the patch of daisies, its engine whirring, stopping, starting. And I was entranced by this small act, this unplanned interruption akin to a last rite.

By the time the ducks lost their beaks in my pain I couldn't talk. I just held Edwin's hand, a revelation in mine. I shrivelled up beside him, like a carcass that had finally stopped tricking people into thinking it could breathe.

Synsepalum

Manu was first spotted in the display window of the old sewing-machine museum touching holes of light on a babushka costume. He seemed to have appeared from nowhere, a pied piper staging gowns as soft instruments, framed by gauzy street lights. His fingers were curled into swathes of the costume's bulbous ruby-red taffeta skirt on a mannequin, surrounded by elaborately designed sewing-machines, poised like an incongruous metal army. A spool of gold thread uncurled behind him, drinking from the night. A wind chime above the blue front door argued with the soft falling of snow. The letterbox slot had a black glove with silver studs slipped into the slash, like a misguided disruption. Manu gripped a large curved needle between his lips, wiped his brow with a spotted handkerchief. The ash in his pockets felt weightless. He inserted the needle into the skirt's hem, unpicking a shrunken, smoggy skyline. He gathered two more mannequins standing to the side, naked, arms stretched towards the skylight in a celestial pose. Their eyes stared ahead blankly, as though fixed on a mirage in the distance that could be broken apart, then fed into their artificial skin, into cloth. He placed them in the display window, naked calling cards waiting to be dressed. The spool of thread cut diagonally across rows of sewing-machines moored on metal stands, rectangular golden plaques identifying each one. There was an antique Singer 66-1 Red Eye Treadle from the 1920s, a Russian Handcrank portable number from the fifties, a 1940s Montgomery Ward Streamliner US model, a compact 1930s Jones model from Bucharest with a silver flower pattern crawling up the sides of its sleek black frame. Manu gathered the thread slowly, a ritual he performed between each creation. A splintered pain exploded in his chest. In his mind's eye, the ash from his pockets assembled into feminine silhouettes. He needed to make more dresses, more corsets, more fitted suits, more gowns. He needed to find more ways to make women feel beautiful through his creations. The designs rose from dark, undulating slipstreams as if in resurrection. They were watery constructions, insistent, whispering what materials they needed, leaning against his brown irises until they leaked from his eyes onto the page while his fingers sketched feverishly. He walked to the atelier at the back, a hub flourishing under the gaze of light. There was a long wooden worktable, more sewing-machines dotted around it. A coiled measuring tape sat in the middle as if ready to entrap a rhinestone-covered, meteorite-shaped white gown that would crash through. Materials spilled from the edges towards the centre: rolls of bright silk, piles of linen, open boxes of lace, streams of velvet. There were jars of accessories, decorations winking in the glass: zips, studs, feathers, small jewelled delights waiting to adorn the pleat of a skirt, the breast of a jacket, dimpled soft satin. A black leather suitcase leaning against one wall spilled tiny grains of invisible sand from its gut. The air's pressure contorted a candy-hued ballerina-style dress carelessly flung over a guillotine.

It was on this night, while leafleting, Noma was drawn to the seductive glow from the museum, orbs of light mutating in the front entrance's bubble of glass, a coloured small window in a door, a geometric code for the eye. A head in the window of that door on a winter's night could appear trapped there, bobbing in the glass curiously. Noma arrived at that moment through a triumvirate of migration from Swaziland to Paris to the UK. Picking fruit to sell on the scorching roads of South Africa, homeless in Paris before working in a toy factory, leafleting in London, which was repetitive, flexible, mundane but easy, bookended by daily returns to her tiny bedsit on the other side of Wandsworth, in a death trap with no fire exits just off the high street. Noma held a roll of leaflets in her right hand, a run of five hundred for a show about a woman trapped in a warehouse encountering a doppelgänger at each exit every time she attempted to leave. She tugged one strap of her rucksack further up her shoulder, walked towards the museum door. Flakes of snow christened her, like a black Venus, in the cold. Spotting the babushka dress in the display window, she pressed her face into the glass partition in the door, intrigued. The door opened. Manu smiled warmly, motioned her in with one hand, a ruffle of taffeta material in the other. It smelt like incense inside. The gentle ring of wind chimes multiplied in her eardrums; the low skyline from the babushka costume bent over the sewing-machines; the pressure of air made her skin hum; her senses were heightened. She felt sucked into a vacuum. Air seeped inside her like helium in the lungs. Mannequins facing the outside had drops of dew in their mouths.

'You have come for work,' Manu announced. His elegantly handsome face was wise in the light. Not even awaiting a response, he turned, rushing to the atelier. Noma trailed after him; the roll of leaflets fell from her hands, becoming confetti in the view from the front door's bubbled-glass partition.

She began working for him a week later, scouring shops for fine materials, measuring and cutting, learning to sew, hunting for unusual accessories. She visited milliners, procured fine hats the colour of quail eggs, the burnished gold of the Sahara, the hue of the Garonne at night. She watched his sketches come to life with a soft wonder in her throat, the outfits like architectural constructs waiting for bodies to invade them, her fingers spinning them slowly on a tailor's mannequin under the kaleidoscopic glow from the skylight, the quiet language of sand stealthily spilling in a corner, the chug of the sewing-machines temporarily silenced. The pop-up atelier in the sewing-machine museum sprang up, like a small Utopia longing for the flurry of action. And the women came like drunken butterflies drawn to Eden, one by one, until the atelier became a hive of activity, leaking laughter and excitable voices. The women were seduced by Manu, his beauty, his sophistication, the unpredictability of his style, his erudite tales and the assured rumble of his voice. He told them he was born in the Gambia, Namibia, Zanzibar. He was inconsistent, flamboyant. *Oh, but where was he from again?* No matter. He offered them Synsepalum, wild African berries, as if the fruit grew from the blade of the guillotine, the hands of the old grandfather clock on one atelier wall, the mouths of the mannequins. The break of sweet, exotic fruit flooded the women's tongues. They kept coming back for more; more Manu, more handfuls of Synsepalum, more Noma, flicking through his sketches, fingering the lines of all they could be, if only. Aspiration captured in drawings. All the while, kernels of pain formed inside Manu, gathering into a mass.

The orders increased. Mrs Jovan, head of the town council, had a nettle-green Boudicca gown made for her, which swished around her ankles romantically; Mrs Lonegran, owner of a chain of flower stores, cooed in pleasure at the final reveal of her metallic Joan of Arc-inspired ensemble on the atelier floor. Mrs Hunt, a wine buyer, blinked at her image in an intricately designed pale off-shoulder 1920s flapper number, with a crystallised beaded beret to match, gasping as if she hadn't seen herself before, at least not in this way. Manu made women feel marvellous, valued, appreciated. He not only understood the female form, he celebrated it: every dip of the back, every arch of a neck, every individual flare of hips. He masked and he revealed, he obscured and he unearthed. He knew how to make the most ordinary of women feel like a goddess. This was his gift. Every woman had a quality of beauty of her own making lurking beneath the skin. Manu knew ways to make it bloom, how to tease it to the surface. And every night, Noma would return to her lonely bedsit bone tired, fall into bed, unceremoniously woken by the leak in her ceiling landing on her face, acting as an alarm for the next day's activities.

Five months passed. The women loved their new outfits. They danced in their hallways wearing them, spun in mirrors gathering mist the colour of Synsepalum. Their reflections were released, mimicking their poses in the poorer areas of town, the other side: a swish of silk skirt passing the window of a Turkish food hall that had shut down, a pantsuit limp against the keyhole of a gutted former Jamaican takeaway, a squeezed flamenco dress sleeve brushing the iron gates of an abandoned youth centre that had lost its funding. Slipstreams followed each reflection, like a watery shadow. By June, the shots of pain Manu experienced had intensified, spreading through his limbs. His hands in particular were in constant pain. He woke up in agony, the fingers appearing gnarled to him. He couldn't keep up with the orders, with the monster he'd created. The rise of sand from the suitcase in the corner of the atelier had become too much. The mannequins were pregnant with mirages; stomachs protruded, splitting material. The glove in the post slot had swelled with blood. Designs from the periphery had begun to crash through the skylight in confused stupors, unsure of how their material versions would manifest. The chug of the sewing-machines in his ears was constant, till he found himself impersonating the sound sporadically in conversation. He'd run out of ash. And his wild African berries no longer grew in the area for him.

On the third occasion the women wore their outfits, they discovered Manu had lied to them. They could wear the designs only three times. The third time, they couldn't get out of them. Seams tightened, buttons couldn't be undone, petticoats became silken cages. The women rolled around in the damp earth of their gardens, climbed onto their husbands, partners, lovers, hollering to them to get the scissors, knives, shears, anything to cut them out. They spilled onto the streets. It was on this morning that Noma arrived outside the museum to find the crowd of women. Manu had disappeared, gone to the next place, the next set of women who needed to feel good, whose images of themselves he could manipulate, like startled adult changelings behind a lens. The atelier was empty, the sewing-machines and mannequins forlorn in the void. Noma spotted something glinting at the foot of the front entrance. She picked up the curved needle. The baying women rounded on her. 'Who will make us beautiful now?' they chorused, like a warped choir on the loose, faces strained, mouths drawn, teeth bared, closing in, scissors and shears gripped firmly, raised above their heads. Noma almost dropped the needle just as the women began to turn to ash, the pads of her fingers sweaty, just as a bright red root bloomed in the eye of the needle.

Zinzi from Boketto

Prussia 1800s

As the light refracted some distance beyond the decorated carriage, Halmin spotted the figure of a woman emerging from its curve: dark-skinned, slender, disoriented, haphazardly dressed in a slip of turquoise cloth with an unusual yellow block pattern. At that time of the night, there were a few finely dressed couples dotted around the narrow street in Pomerania walking arm in arm, heads bobbing under the glow of streetlamps, which softened them in the cold while they passed shops and establishments closed for the evening, the gold lettering in store windows illuminated, the bells above their entrances silenced by the quiet language of the dark. Sheets of snow fell at angles, lightly dusting rooftops. The sharp, rhythmic sound of the horses' hoofs punctuated the whistling night air. A haggard-looking hound dashed across the street as if chasing a blood moon round corners. Halmin's left hand twitched. The horses became jittery the closer they got to the woman, twisting their faces, groaning in protest, spittle flying from their mouths as he tugged at the reins to combat the sudden tension in his hands. He sat up, a few ragged breaths leaving his body, adjusted his top hat, an action to ground him, remove him from the unpredictability of the moment but it didn't. He gripped the reins tightly. The woman glimmered, wobbled, rippled in the heart of a cold snap, as if transported from another dimension. He had witnessed something like this before, several years back travelling through desert country, where the heat was so intense you could see a half-formed version of yourself reaching up to you from a puddle before you blinked it away. He had never seen something like this in Prussia, not in the provinces he had passed through. They called it an apparition, a mirage, a trick of light, a vision from the margins planted within a man's reach to run his fingers over, to dip and pull disintegrating items from. The mirage woman was only a few steps away, occasionally flicking her tongue over lips to leave its moist cavern and curl above their heads like a stunted pink flag. She was slightly pigeon-toed, which gave her movements a distinctive air, a trait Halmin often sought. Her hair was braided in a way he had never seen in Prussia: close to the scalp with spaces in between, the ends brushing her shoulders. Her face was open, possessing a regal look. It was the way she raised her head, how she held his gaze unwaveringly, despite her body shivering before bursting into action. She stuck her arms out, bent her knees in a confrontational stance almost forcing the horses to respond. And, of course, they did. Rising up as though ready to break from the carriage of squealing oddities to scour the rooftops for iridescent particles of past nights the woman had left behind, while the carriage was sucked into the vortex, Halmin reduced to a mouth in his top hat and the woman using the reins to drag people from the carriage into sudden embraces.

She cooed, clicking her tongue, reaching into the pocket of her garment for two radish-coloured lumps. She offered them to the horses, which slowly started to settle, before nuzzling her palms as though they had been doing it for years, sliding the two sweet lumps into their mouths in swift movements. She rubbed their heads, her breaths like puffs of mist. Her throat constricted. Her collar bones were prominent in the angle of light, weapons lodged beneath the skin. She looked behind her, unable to mask a fleeting, harried expression. It was clear to Halmin that, wherever she had come from, this woman was running from something.

'Zinzi!' she announced, patting her chest insistently with her left hand.

'Back!' Halmin ordered curtly. 'Stay back.' He made the action to charge at her but the horses wouldn't follow suit. She showed him her pockets, raising her arms slowly, understanding perfectly what was unsaid. Across the street, a man wearing a white cravat, which flopped at his neck like a restless companion, puffed on his pipe, eyeing them suspiciously. Another, holding a silver-tipped cane he used in an exaggerated fashion, watched them as he passed but made no move to intervene. Halmin steered the carriage to the side. The woman followed. He assessed her discreetly: the smooth richness of her skin, the whiteness of her half-smile stark in contrast, high cheekbones, liquid brown eyes with flecks of gold, sad eyes, despite the awkward smile. He suddenly felt the tiredness seeping into his core. There was a bitter taste in his mouth. His knuckles were raw and bruised from fighting two men earlier who had not wanted to pay after the show. His jaw ached. A thudding rang in his head, like a series of knocks in floating matter, the imprints of a hand at work he could not see. There was no doubt he was in a terrible mood and had wanted to drink himself to sleep but this woman alone on a wintry night had interfered with that and he was not completely without empathy. He hopped off the horse, beckoned the woman close. His hawkish features pronounced, he asked, 'Do you trust a stranger's word?'

Her shoulders rose; watching him carefully, she shook her head. This amused Halmin. He chuckled, his large frame momentarily less threatening. He noted the green bracelet on her right ankle, the weathered shoes on her feet not dissimilar to balletic footwear but completely inappropriate for the outside.

'Do you have a bed this evening?'

She shook her head, an annoyed expression on her face as though irritated to have found herself in this position.

'Oh, we may not be the Château de Compiègne, Mademoiselle,' Halmin spat, 'but a bed is a bed.' He walked her round to the back of the carriage. 'I will not lay a finger upon your person.' He opened it, ushering her in. 'You have company in there,' he said, smiling wolfishly, eyes gleaming. 'Welcome to Heaven.'

He closed the back. She found herself being assessed by several pairs of eyes. The horses' hoofs clicked. The carriage began to move steadily. She sat down gingerly, her eyes scanning the contained space. A flame-haired woman with a replica head protruding from her stomach nodded, a blush spreading across her cheeks. Two conjoined dwarfs playing the maracas with miserable expressions eyed her grudgingly, wary of any new person. 'Where has this fine lady been dragged from?' they asked, almost in unison, maracas limp in their hands.

'Zinzi,' she said, offering her name as a way of breaking the tension.

'Never heard of such a place.' The dwarfs sneered, the cruel expressions on their faces tightening.

In the opposite corner sat a hunchback man with red-rimmed eyes who kept glancing at Zinzi shyly. His forehead was elongated as though he'd recently passed a trick mirror, inheriting a distorted version of himself. His brown shirt sleeves were rolled up. There were faint scratches on his arms. He held a bright orange parrot with tufts springing from its head that kept screeching, 'Happy birthday! Happy birthday!' The parrot belonged to Halmin. Zinzi was left somewhat confused: apparently not one of them had seen a birthday in months. The hunchback gently ran a finger over the parrot's head. The carriage jerked. Halmin clicked his tongue at the horses. Zinzi thought she saw the passing man's cravat transformed into a one-winged bird rushing at the scratches on the hunchback's arms, at the secrets behind it, before glinting between them all. She took a deep breath to steady the uneasiness she felt. Her throat constricted. She was thirsty and hungry. Her skin was cold. She shivered a little. There was an aching in both knees, as if her body had retained the memory of covering miles and miles. She peeked through the gaps in the carriage: more lightly frosted pathways, the silhouettes of dark candle-sticks in windows of large houses, pale people with strange formal clothing that seemed to restrict their movements somewhat, particularly the women. Her eyes swam. She thought back to waking after seeing a man's hands reaching for a large wooden chest, folding her naked limbs into it, tossing it in choppy white waters, the chest tumbling inside the sea while she screamed. And the sea's creatures floated above the coppery lock and chain, bright and bewildered, as if something had been lost in translation. Then the seabed shed bits of itself to meet a woman in a watery decline, her sense of hope completely diminished. Splintered bits of light came, so blindingly hot it broke the chest open, scattering intoxicated sea life into a spell of erratic flight.

On the carriage ride, Zinzi discovered that the hunchback was called Tiny, the parrot Flaubert, the flame-haired woman and her replica head the two Estrellas, and the conjoined dwarfs were the Gustav brothers, Roman and Émile. They stopped their vexing maracas-playing briefly so Émile could fling one at Flaubert, who had not stopped giving birthday wishes all journey. Flaubert's response was to flap around the carriage in a frenzy, squealing, 'Unfair, sir! Unfair, *en garde!*' And a small burst of laughter rang through the carriage until Halmin, as if waiting to stifle any enjoyment or joy, barked, 'Quiet back there! Or I shall relish throwing every single one of you useless monstrosities off this carriage. Aha! Let's see how you survive without Halmin! Nobody will have you. Why, even the parrot is worth more than all of you combined,' he jeered, in a tone that dared any of them to argue back. 'Who wants to try their luck fending for themselves?' he asked. 'No takers? No takers, Flaubert! Ha-ha.' He steered the carriage around a corner. The horses picked up the pace as though the devil himself had run his tongue over the cracks in their heels. Zinzi abruptly slid to one side from the tug of movement, knocking into Estrella while Estrella Two blinked rapidly. Somebody's stomach rumbled and Zinzi could not tell if it was hers since she was a little faint.

She felt somewhat outside herself, as though observing everything with an odd resignation, a sense of inevitability. The Gustav brothers played cards with each other for the rest of the journey; Tiny hummed as he built a stickman; Estrella brushed the red locks of Estrella Two, who sighed in satisfaction. Flaubert retreated to one side of Tiny, his back to them in a huff. After the carriage eventually pulled to a stop, Halmin hit the back, indicating they had reached their destination. One by one they jumped out. Flaubert fluttered onto his shoulder. Halmin bowed dramatically. 'Welcome to the Palace of Versailles.' Flaubert hopped up and down on his shoulder in excitement. Zinzi homed in on Halmin, on his attire, wondering about the shadows dancing in his eyes, the gold buttons that had abandoned his handsome red coat.

The Palace of Versailles turned out to be a series of dilapidated plots by the canal at the edge of Pomerania where the vagabonds, miscreants and society's unwanted languished in harmonious decay. Halmin could be a miserable bastard but he was not without humour. Zinzi lingered beside him uncertainly.

'What is your trick?' he asked, pointing at the cluster of outliers he managed. 'Every single one of them can do something for me. There is no free passage here.' His lips curled into a sneer; the shadows in his eyes danced.

'Zinzi no trick,' she said, with a confused expression.

'Zinzi go far,' she answered, using both hands, like she was reaching for something beyond them, into another horizon, past the cold land she had found herself in. The others glanced at her pityingly before sharing a knowing look.

Halmin grabbed Zinzi by the arm. The suddenness of the action threw her. 'Well, I suppose the sight of you is enough to fascinate people,' he offered, almost softly, his eyes running over her features. 'But we shall have to unearth some hidden talent. Come, come! I have a whore and a jug of beer to attend to in no particular order.'

Poor people in various states of disarray milled about an ironically designed courtyard. A man moved around awkwardly with one foot that had turned green. An exhausted-looking woman held a wailing baby to her breasts. Several men were gathered playing a game with stones, laughing, erupting into short bursts of conversation, noticing the new arrivals. Another group of people were congregated by a robust fire on the periphery, the cinders flickering, the flames curling as if a dragon would leap out and lose bits of itself in their pockets. Halmin walked ahead, whistling; his beleaguered troupe followed. To the amusement of the people around, Flaubert flapped his wings, yelling, 'Man fire! Man fire!'

The troupe were weary. Their limbs ached from a long evening of travel and a longer day of work. Halmin was unsympathetic, impatient. 'Hurry, I have no time for this dawdling. Must the elements be aligned for you ungrateful creatures to show some appreciation? Move!' He ushered them inside the plot. The last they saw of him that night was his large, intimidating figure standing by the entrance as though bracing himself against something, a batch of keys dangling from his left hand, a rakish smile that almost made him handsome, his top hat in a jaunty angle, as though a skyline would emerge, blinding them momentarily in an offering of respite.

The plot itself, one of several, was cold and a little damp. Halmin had deliberately not fed them that evening so their stomachs continued to rumble. The air smelt stale. The patter of their footsteps echoed. A few wooden crates were scattered around, like makeshift beds. They each gravitated towards one. Several barrels were stashed in a corner coated with specks of dust. There were neither cloths nor blankets to cover themselves with and the temperature was dropping. They would have to make do with their body warmth alone, which was insufficient. Cracks ran across the ceiling, crisscrossing in short trails. The sound of a toad harrumphing from behind one barrel filled the space, a warped clarion in their midst.

'That is all we need!' Émile whined. 'How are we supposed to sleep with that creature in here?'

Roman added, 'I am going to gouge out the eyes of the formerly great Halmin one day. Right after I cook his trusted Flaubert over a fire!'

'The toad is life among us,' Estrella declared. Estrella Two nodded in agreement.

As if it had been called to interruption, the toad wandered from behind the barrels, leaping between the crates in short, quick bursts. Zinzi watched its jumps, its skin moving like mottled green silk in the darkness, its eyes filmy, as though it carried a morning to come inside them. She pictured water lilies waiting to bloom in the spots it had touched.

'Estrella, your sentimentality never fails to be underwhelming,' Roman said, wearing an irritated expression.

'Well, I like it,' Tiny responded, a scowl on his face. He turned his large body, his bulbous back challenging the Gustav brothers to argue with him.

'I hope the whore saps every last ounce of his energy,' Émile said, flicking lint from his teeth.

'If he returns having spent all his money he will be in a foul mood.' Estrella slumped on her crate; a frightened look crossed her eyes. Estrella Two yawned. Zinzi lay down, staring up at the stained, cracked ceiling. The wood was hard against her back. She wrung her hands anxiously as the noise from outside filtered through, like a looming discontent seeping in. After the others fell asleep and the toad had settled somewhere temporary, she heard soft crying. It was Tiny. She could almost feel his back moving up and down in the dark, as if the tears were coming from his hump. She wandered over to him, careful not to wake the others, leaving her last radish-coloured sweet on his crate.

The next day, Halmin returned with a loaf of Vollkorn bread for them. They rushed off their crates at the sound of the plot door key turning slowly in the lock. The door slid open. Flaubert was perched on Halmin's shoulder, a tiny piece of bread stuck in his beak. The bright tufts on his head had been flattened with a finger of Halmin's hair pomade.

'The day awaits us and maybe a little fortune along the way,' Halmin announced. 'Come, come!' They ate like starved scavengers. Zinzi had never tasted this type of bread before. It was thick and dry with an earthy flavour and the seeds got stuck in her teeth.

Afterwards, they washed around the back. Zinzi and the two Estrellas shared a bucket of cold water, behind a hung cloth Halmin provided to give them privacy. Estrella Two complained about the water getting into her eyes, the shadow of her head visible in the cloth, undulating, as though waiting for the creases in the white sheet to produce other parts of a body for her. Then it was practice time inside the plot, away from the prying eyes of others and the crates moved aside. Halmin offloaded their various props from the back of the carriage. He moved from one to another, shouting and commenting in a tone of frustration, barking at the Gustav brothers, 'Look like you're enjoying it!' as they fiddled with their accordion.

'Higher note, higher at the end, Estrellas,' he said tersely, listening to them sing. 'Nothing you do should ever be ordinary. There is no glory from past performances. There is only the one now and the one ahead of you.'

He simply paced around Tiny, who was lifting heavy items, balancing them on his shoulders with ease. The tension between them was fraught with contained fury. Halmin watched his every movement bearing a scornful expression, his jaw working, his brow furrowed.

By the time he came to Zinzi she knew he would expect something from her. She did not want to anger the man who might be able to help her in some way. Estrella One had loaned her a spare set of pantaloons so she was warmer, more comfortable. Halmin stood so close to her she could feel the heat off his body. And Flaubert was fluttering around between them all, like a ringmaster in waiting. She somersaulted, the way she had learned to as a girl.

'Well, well, the stranger from the night has tricks up her borrowed pantaloons,' Halmin said. She could not tell if he was pleased.

'Wait here,' he ordered, heading off to the carriage. He returned clutching a large red hoop he held out to her. 'For your act,' he instructed softly, smiling.

'Act?' Zinzi replied, her confusion apparent. The others gathered around her.

'Yes!' Halmin answered. 'You are a natural. And the

troupe could do with some new energy.' He grinned mischievously, as though he had just drawn blood.

By evening, Zinzi watched in wonder as Halmin converted the back of the carriage into a stage. And a bright blue sign was placed at the top that read *Halmin's Circus Wonders*. Halmin had procured a golden leotard for her to wear, along with a matching short pleated skirt, which complimented her skin, the material fluttering against her thighs. The two Estrellas helped, adding touches to fit the occasion, with Estrella One assisting and Estrella Two commenting on adjustments, her head protruding from Estrella One's stomach in excitement, her face flushed. They added a bit of silver sparkle to Zinzi's arms and black kohl around her eyes to accentuate their almond-shaped beauty, a dab of rouge with hints of gold on both cheeks; lastly bright multi-coloured threads added to her braids, immediately drawing the eye to her distinctive crown. She was resplendent, other-worldly, elegant.

Zinzi suspected Halmin approved because his only comment upon seeing her after removing the cigar from his mouth was, 'Do not damage the carriage.' The pulse in his cheek throbbed; the cleft in his jaw left a groove slight enough for a breath to kiss. 'No injuries tonight,' he added, almost as an afterthought. 'Not on your debut, at least.' He ran a finger over one line of purple thread in her hair. A tingling sensation crawled up her spine. She lingered behind the carriage, nervously watching the others as the large crowds gathered. Halmin's displays always drew a mixture of society, both the underclass and the wealthy, expensively attired with a taste for the more bizarre acts. Protests had occurred earlier that day in the province from workers' unions in a handful of regions in Prussia regarding unsatisfactory wages, and there had been arguments in Parliament about how these disruptions should be tackled. And so the crowds were eager to be entertained as the light pooled on the carriage stage.

One by one they performed. The Gustav brothers, garishly made up, played the maracas and the accordion, interspersed with pithy social commentary on Prussia's predicament and political mishaps, which made the audience chuckle. Then the two Estrellas sang operatic sonnets, which were equally unsettling and captivating. Tiny came on in a red striped wrestler's outfit, balancing heavy items on top of his back, his hump accentuated to look even more outlandish, as if one-eyed creatures grew inside, reaching for their lost sight. When Zinzi came on, the crowd gasped. A ripple of shock passed through it, followed by murmurs. She began to move, her spins and tumbles landing with the odd little imperfections that gave her a signature style. She used the hoop inventively, rolling through it, spinning it on her ankles, throwing it above her head to catch it in a split position. Zinzi danced to a rhythm they had never seen, so charged that the excitement in the air was infectious.

And Halmin, not one to miss an opportunity, walked through the crowd with Flaubert on one shoulder, his hat outstretched as people reached into their pockets, throwing in coins. Finally Zinzi surprised the audience and Halmin with her final move, contorting her body completely, flinging her legs over her head and scuttling along the stage floor on her hands, like a rare, beautifully adorned beetle.

Flaubert flew off Halmin's shoulder, hopping up and down beside his hat on the ground. 'Zinzi!' Flaubert warbled. 'You are a wonder, you are a wonder!' And the crowd roared rapturously.

Word spread about the exciting new addition to Halmin's troupe. Zinzi unsurprisingly had several admirers, men who returned again and again to see her, much to Halmin's chagrin. As long as they paid for the show, he never commented. They performed all around the province. Halmin continued to push Zinzi to do more contortion as part of her act, so she did, manipulating her body into bizarre shapes audiences could not believe, sometimes in pain after pushing her limbs beyond limits. She repeatedly insisted she needed to go home but Halmin kept delaying helping her. 'Home? Look at the following you have in Prussia. The troupe is making more money than it has for a long time. Do you consider me a madman?' he said, gesticulating irritably.

Like any group who spent a great amount of time together,

there were occasional rumblings. The two Estrellas argued over who got to sing lead for one or two songs.

Estrella One had to sing by herself for several nights in a row while Estrella Two, hair lank and unbrushed, looked at the crowds glumly, red-faced. The Gustav brothers, fed up of playing the maracas, demanded new instruments to no avail, blamed each other, hurled insults but neither of them could storm off dramatically since they were conjoined. Tiny continued to weep sometimes at night. He never confided in Zinzi, although she encouraged him when she could, when her mind was not dwelling too much on her own secrets, sitting beside him wordlessly, leaving her hand on his shoulder until she felt the trembling subside. Flaubert got a cold and did not speak for three days, a strange experience for all of them. They missed his screeching and oddly jumbled commentary. That period, he took to raising his head to the sky mournfully, as though its darker shapes would crash to quieten all their tongues. After one show, Zinzi saw Halmin shouting at Tiny behind the carriage. Tiny's head was bowed meekly. She could not make out the argument properly due to the cheer and buzz of the crowds spilling around them, though she made a promise to herself to check on Tiny later.

Some evenings, Halmin scoured the slums for castaways in search of a new member to join the troupe. He was particular. For a man whose income relied on presenting the unimaginable, they had to be just right. And, of course, Halmin was his stage name. He was in the business of illusion, tricks, the bizarre and a name that suggested the exotic, the darkness of the unknown was fitting. He had been born Theodore Husdvt in a small town west of Prussia to a ruinous log-seller father and a hapless cotton-mill-working mother. By the time he became the great ringmaster Halmin, years later, he had left most of that behind, his memories fracturing in the folds of history. At its peak, the great Halmin's circus had performed for the highest of the land, entertaining princes, parliamentary members, foreign envoys in decadent halls, lush gardens, courtyards crafted by the country's finest architects. Other than sex, there was no greater thrill for him than the power he held over both an audience and his acts, moulding the needs of one to suit the other. Even in those instances when he saw things he should not have: dwarfs carrying stomach entrails up to audience members, a woman jester impaled on a spike with the flowers of spring bursting from her mouth, a head wailing in the ring, which became a weeping wound. It had made sense that the symmetry of his acts would spawn uncomfortable scenes of their own, waiting to pass through his chest, taking shelter there when they needed to. After the scandal broke, he was cast out from that world, losing everything, back on the streets. Along the way, he had often thought of those moneyed, esteemed folk turning their backs on him. They were carcasses in luxurious outfits, reaching for the concavities in his body in order to breathe. Halmin had stumbled around in the dark, bruising that past version of himself again and again because he needed to. As for the scandal, he had done what had to be done, which was to take an abomination from the blood, then hold it up to the corrosive edges of the world.

Six months passed. Zinzi picked up some of the dialect, Frisian in particular, from listening to the troupe and audience members. On the night Halmin came to her, it was after a performance at the Sigmaringen Inn. She was sitting in her dressing room removing her bracelets when he walked in. There had been an increasing tension between them since she had joined the troupe. She felt a ribbon of heat uncurling in her stomach. A tight expression flashed across his face. He bore a haunted look in his eyes. He kneeled before her, held her gaze. 'I need you tonight, do you understand? I want to please you in the way a man does for a woman.' He rested his hands on her thighs, a gentle proclamation. The warmth from them spread right to her core. She slipped her hand into his thick dark hair, running her fingers over his head in a way he had not thought he needed. 'Zinzi know. I understand,' she murmured.

Halmin tasted like nectar and poison all at once, like a sweet seed, then a sharp object searching her mouth for a place to cut. The room swam. Light from her performance earlier in the evening bobbed in the mirror. The urgency of the movements from their bodies caused a spillage of kohl on the mauve dresser littered with adornments, a black snake of disruption dribbling onto the floor. Colourful costumes hanging to the side shimmered. Small illusions from each performance shrank in the corner of the room, threatening their resurrection in other contained spaces.

On the floor, a red throw billowed underneath them. They undressed. Halmin noticed lighter short lines on her hips. He paused a moment. A crackle of electricity filled the air. He ran a finger over them. Wherever Zinzi had come from, she had left a child behind. He turned away from that realisation, away from the secrets they all carried with them. He buried his head between her legs, his tongue lapping at her greedily. She lifted her hips as though she would come right off the throw, arched her back.

'Halmin, I must go home. When can I go?' she asked.

'Stop saying that!' he barked. 'Do you not enjoy the applause? What I have given you? Do you think you can do this without me?' He was so annoyed by her resolve to keep asking him, by her ridiculous sense of timing, he slipped inside her to stop the thoughts swimming in his head, moaning, kissing her tenderly. The noise from outside faded. A silver headdress had fallen off the dresser, landing in the small pool of kohl. Halmin was feral in that light, teeth bared, expression twisted. His head thrown back, driven by a primal instinct, looming above, then changing into one bright wing travelling inside her.

*

Over the ensuing months the group travelled even more as the demand for their shows grew. They performed across Stettin. Halmin worked them harder, pushing their bodies beyond what they had thought was possible. Sometimes they did three shows in one evening. They spent their days practising or locked away. Halmin did not allow them to form bonds or any close relationships. If he observed signs of that, he would speed up their departure from an area. He was eagle-eyed and relentless. He drank more. His dark moods increased away from the eyes of others. Not that people cared enough about what happened to his 'band of freaks', as he called them, almost affectionately. They were entertained by them, studied them, and were endlessly curious about those they considered society's oddities, but they were rarely given full consideration or empathy. Halmin had even negotiated with a physician from Sweden who had seen one of their shows that he would give him the Gustav brothers to dissect for a fee should an unfortunate accident happen to them.

Zinzi continued to intrigue him, yet Halmin told himself you never let a woman in. You kept her close enough for your bed but far from your heart. You tried to break her, slowly if necessary. You made sure she had no hold, no power over you, that her grip on you, or what she imagined you to be, kept slipping, her feet trapped in quicksand, her body beholden to yours. But Zinzi was spirited, temperamental. And secretly after each show he panicked, a feeling of dread knotting in his stomach.

She was not like the others. He knew that. He had seen it, after all.

When Zinzi went for a walk with an admirer of hers after a show one night, Flaubert alerted him, flapping at him in a panic with the two Estrellas gaunt from hunger unsuccessfully trying to silence him. 'Zinzi, come back!' Flaubert yelped.

'Who does she think she is? Marie Antoinette?' the Gustav brothers remarked drily.

Halmin was furious. He found Zinzi and dragged her back to their site. He considered her dalliance an act of rebellion, nearly throttling her, his hands at her throat as she kicked, scratched and screamed. It was Tiny who saved her, lifting Halmin off her body as though he weighed nothing. People huddled around like droves of insects.

'No, brother, stop!' Tiny said; his expression was full of intent. 'Let her be,' he insisted. There was anger in his voice and a steeliness nobody had expected.

Halmin turned deathly pale. His eyes bulged, as though they would pop out of his head. 'Never call me that!' he spat, lips thinning. 'I'll kill you,' he warned, before walking away. Zinzi sat up shaking, breathless, tears formed. She looked up at Tiny, thanking him quietly. They shared a silent exchange, his revelation of being Halmin's sibling hanging between them, like a barbed thread. She thought back to past moments that now made sense: Tiny's crying while the others slept was a constant mourning for a

brotherly relationship he would never get, his loyalty to
Halmin, despite Halmin's being physically capable of harm-
ing him, his naked desire for Halmin's approval, the way
he would discreetly break, then put himself back together
when Halmin did not acknowledge his efforts on the
stage. And then there was Halmin's equal fascination and
contempt for difference. It was deep within him, a gnarled
thing losing its teeth in his blood.

They were on their way to the district of Schivelbein when
the road forked into two. The distance at the end of it on
the right hand side began to glimmer. Zinzi peeked through
the carriage, catching her breath. Another world was
reflected back: this time it was a large ship in the dock. She
had seen the chest there. She had clutched at a red tide in
its waters. The light from there was bending. She knew she
had to get to it. She knew that, on the other side, Halmin's
world would be reduced to another marking on her hip.
Heat spread through her, like a lick of wildfire curling
through a vein. The horses reared. The two Estrellas cried
out from the carriage jerking. The Gustav brothers, Roman
and Émile, were stunned into silence for once. Tiny started
rocking back and forth, looking around anxiously. Zinzi
jumped out of the carriage, rushing towards that ship with
every ounce of will she possessed. Halmin was screaming
for her to stop. The air crackled. The night expanded. The
sky's constellations caved at their corners. Prussia gleamed

dark and forlornly. Flaubert flew out, following her, flapping ahead into the distance, only to split into two at the point of entry, one half of him silenced on the road, the other falling onto the ship's mast. Halmin's voice echoed in Zinzi's ears as she fled. She did not look back because this other world beckoned, glistening seductively as though it was newly born, forged for her recalibration, rising from a deceptively softened edge.

Dune Dunelm

How the fossil arrived in the trap remained a mystery to him, even moments later. But in that instant Canelo approached it the way one might when experiencing divinity for the first time: in wonder, respectfully, slowly, barely feeling his feet crossing the ground. The creak of movements from the trap punctuated the low cacophony of sound, the trembling of surrounding trees, the scent of an exotic nectar in his nostrils, a chasm in the air his body sensed but couldn't locate, the landing of something bright and fractured to the left of his vision. And, of course, what appeared to be a fossil at first. It looked like a Fulgurite born from lightning on sand. It was iridescent, undulating slowly as if testing its confines, the nubs on the spine distending then retracting in efficient movements, a dance of one in a cage. *Nieto, what have you discovered?* the ancestors chimed in his ears. *What is that sound coming from it?* A shot of adrenalin rippled through him, making him hyper-alert, the way a person might become sensing potential danger or in flight mode. He stopped midway; as though attuned to the rhythm of his movements, the fossil paused too. In the short haze that followed, he traced his activities back, trying to ascertain what he'd done to make this happen: some ridge, opening or bending of infinity he'd inadvertently triggered to enable this entity to slip through.

Two days before, there had been the boat ride, an hour across the water to get to Rapa Nui Island in Chile, not far from Tahiti. And the boatman having made that trip on plenty of occasions understood the importance of tranquillity for passengers, saying very little unless Canelo asked him a question. The sinews of his arms strained as he rowed, the rhythmic slicing of the oars in the water, his weathered, fairly average-looking face arranged into a calm expression, a barely audible whistle coming from his lips. Canelo's throat was dry on the ride over, as though the boat had its own weather and the boatman was a kind of weather conductor. He'd swallowed his anxiety, pushing it back into the parts of himself that seemed unknowable, even to him. His backpack wedged between his knees, he fiddled with the black Casio watch in his pocket, aware of its imprint on his left wrist. He was a stranger on a boat with another stranger: what could be better? His gaze took in the large thirteenth-century moai statues erected around, the wide expanse of water, imagining the ascent of creatures below, as if they had answers for him. On arrival, he briefly wandered through the small lodge available for use, then set up camp outside in the forest near the waters. He liked the sound of it at night and the possibilities of what it could bring his way, like oddly shaped entities from the body balancing precariously on rafts spinning in curtains of mist, a broken amulet washed up on the sand, a perforated puppet limp against the line between the land and the waters, the sky swirling as though in contemplation. He'd unpacked: clothes, some condiments, reading material including a copy of Bessie Head's *A Collector of Treasures*, Maximilian Voloshin's slim volume of poems and Voltaire's *Candide*. He set up his blue tent efficiently, in a fairly discreet area not too far from the lodge, a fine sheen of sweat covering his skin, the heat off his wiry body a small comfort, the ticking of his brain awaiting translucent wings to attach themselves to it, to transport it elsewhere in his body, perhaps the lung, the intestine or a strip of cartilage. In the lodge, he found a shovel, cooking utensils, blankets, chopped wood and the animal trap shaped like a cage tucked behind an oil drum in the kitchen, which was an odd place to leave it. But Canelo didn't think on this for too long. The air had got into his system. He felt himself opening up to the vision he'd played in his mind's eye, embracing it fully. He caught Rapa Nui fish, brought a compact table from the lodge out to the edge of the water, along with the shovel and a knife. The waters lapped at his feet. He placed the fish on the table, silvery sacrificial deities staring blankly at the distance.

He dug a pit to cook, just like his father had taught him,

the way they had cooked many times when he was a child, the way they cooked on Rapa Nui, which made him feel connected to the land. Perhaps there was some alchemy in the digging, in the rupture he caused within the ground, in the warm temperature of air, his shirtless body arched in the pit digging, which contributed to what was to come later. He cleaned the fish, salted it, added a few drops of lemon. That was all it needed for its true flavour to emerge. He wrapped it in clay, sliced three days' worth of potatoes, placed it all in the pit, creating layers with stones and broad leaves before lighting it. A spillage occurred, the water into his brain or the malfunctions from his head into the water, which could accost him from any direction while he waved the knife frantically, fruitlessly, deep in the water and the gleam from the blade catching reflections before distorting them. He blinked the image away. The Manutara gulls above squawked like vultures, rapidly hurtling towards him before swooping away, then landing elegantly on the sand. He swayed from the satisfaction of his labours, out in the wilds the way it should be. His chest was full of Manutara squawks and a language yet to come, his hands aching from the dig, poised to take the next offerings he could mould, trace and whisper to through his fingers before the rhapsody of the knife's tip. Later, he set the trap. And sitting outside the tent, watching for winking constellations, he pictured the trap filling with signal smoke from the pit.

*

He lifted the trap carefully by the handle at the top from the hollow of soil, sun-stroked leaves scattered in its wake. The fossil made a sound not dissimilar to an owl, a deep, distinct call, which echoed in their immediate vicinity. *Oh, my God*, he mumbled, *where have you come from?* It was disconcerting, as if he was hearing his own voice separated from his body, as though he needed to hear his internal commentary out loud to acknowledge what was happening. The fossil cooed in response to his question. The reverberations shot up his arms. He became acutely aware of every movement carrying it back towards the tent, the weight of the trap in his hand, the way it spun a little if he walked too quickly, too eagerly so he settled into a steady pace, the stick of tobacco in his shirt pocket moving, his soiled maroon-coloured T-shirt clinging to the pool of sweat on his back, the tension in his limbs growing. The air crackled, a rush of heat hit his face, as if the chasm he'd felt earlier was moving right beside him. There were silvery rivulets at the bottom of the trap, which must have come from the Fulgurite or the patch of dampened ground where he'd laid the trap. He resisted the urge to touch it, to see if the colour remained the same on his fingers. He wondered if he'd slept through the ground trembling the night before. He couldn't have: he would have roused to that kind of thing, his body usually more aware in new surroundings. It was sliding back and forth which was an odd sensation; he felt acutely attuned to it. How was that even possible? A moving fossil? One that was alive and beating. If it was even a fossil, maybe it just looked like one. And were there others of its kind, buried at different points in the ground, breathing, murmuring and communicating to each other, bleeding silver through the ecosystem below the ground's surface. He was fifty miles out from the nearest village. The area hadn't been flagged up to him as a place for fossil sightings. In fact, the boatman Bastian, whom he'd instructed to return for him in exactly three weeks, hadn't mentioned it at all. He'd only briefly asked whether Canelo had enough batteries for his torch, that it was one of the things people often forgot, he'd said, chuckling. The cavity in one stained front tooth suddenly seemed too conspicuous, cavernous even, like you couldn't trust what he said. It occurred to Canelo that maybe that was why he didn't say much. He was embarrassed about his teeth. Canelo had nodded in response, adjusting himself, looking at the land where a strange shape on the cliff glimmered: a man was pulling stethoscopes from the water before disintegrating while the boatman's head became one large blackened cavity.

Canelo gripped the trap tightly, worried he would drop it from the rush of excitement spreading through his body. He looked behind him: there was nobody there. He was alone as intended. He'd done it out of precaution, selfishness, not wanting to share the moment with anyone. He didn't know what the right first action to take was. He followed the trail back to the tent, which he could see up ahead, its pinched tip, dimpled frame, the flap partially unzipped. He glanced at the trap. The Fulgurite made that cooing sound again, non-threateningly, as if in approval. When he reached the tent area, he placed the trap on the ground, carefully slid its door open, the sound of iron scraping against iron like a warped instrument, the corroded edges coppery. He felt a splinter of pain in his head. The ruptures waiting on the periphery leaned against his irises, ready to bloom behind headaches. The Fulgurite slid out of the trap, expanding, aware of the room it now had again. The way the light hit it at an angle, it appeared to have fallen from the sky. He thought back to the strange shape he'd seen on the cliff in the boat on the way over, octopus-like, and whether there was any correlation. Further to his right, several yards behind the tent, there were three abandoned rusted water tanks, which had once been cobalt blue. At the opposite end was a giant shell with entrances at either side that looked sculptural, alien-like. The land rose behind it in beautiful green swells. The surroundings were shimmering in the heat. As if the images he'd found himself in the middle of would rotate into something else, the chasm revealing itself to be an invisible quarry, the pit filled with the silhouettes of past visitors eating broad green leaves, giant insects taking shade in the water tanks. A film of sweat covered his nose; watery beads dotted his armpits.

The pulse in his temples hummed. He looked up. Zigzag patterns of white filled the sky with a short procession of birds passing through. The headache he'd anticipated was now throbbing familiarly, a nagging companion. He looked down, watching in a kind of drunken disbelief. The Fulgurite was closer. It had lengthened and felt a hair's breath away. The cooing he'd momentarily got used to changed. Now it was shrieking in discomfort as if its form was transitioning again. Canelo's mouth turned desert dry. Its spine became more defined. The nubs shrank back into the skin. What sounded like bones setting rang out. Arms and legs sprouted, breasts. A feminine face appeared, the expression pained then seductive, then curious. Her skin was taut, her features elegant, her hips wide. She was naked and resplendent in the light. She stood unsteadily at first, the way a new calf might, walking towards him, making that owl sound again. Canelo couldn't move. *Panic attack! Panic attack!* he yelled, slapping his face twice, barely breathing. The woman, the changeling, halted before him merely inches away. She mimicked his expression. *Panic attack! Panic attack!* she repeated, slapping her face twice exactly, copying the inflections in his voice, the element of fear that was inescapable, the pitch and breathlessness. Canelo tripped over the skipping rope he'd brought out earlier, coiled and poised to fell him, like a poisoned undercurrent.

*

They called him *el chef deambulando*, the rambling chef. In San Basilio de Palenque, the Afro-Colombian town where he'd been born, where his father cooked pork belly in a pit and Rondon while drinking Neque and telling him ancestors' stories, the seeds had been sown. His father used to say, Hijo, *listen to the instinct the land plants in you, listen to its call. You have the ear of the wild inside you. It is like breathing*, hijo, *you must pay attention to it*. And so he did. He left Colombia at nineteen, determined to make something of himself, leaving behind a broken-hearted mother and five siblings, three brothers, two sisters, and the suffocating provincial shortcomings of township life. He had a hunger and curiosity about the world that propelled him forward, the ancestors' stories breaking and re-forming in his pockets, between heartbeats. He went to Mexico City first; afterwards he headed to Vienna. There he pounded the streets looking for work but doors were shut in his face. He didn't speak the language at first, which made things difficult. He was an outsider, dynamic, chatty and very expressive. It wasn't the European way. He had to learn when to dial down aspects of himself if necessary. One day, he knocked on the door of a restaurant called Amano, Amano! run by an Italian chef named Molinari, who informed him there were no openings for work, but Canelo kept coming back. Molinari was quietly impressed by his determination. One evening, after the restaurant had just shut, he let him in. He was charming, this Canelo. He commented on things he'd noticed about the restaurant's menu and its customers that even his staff hadn't picked up on. He was handsome too, similar to Basquiat in looks. Molinari was fascinated by his raw energy, his passion for food, his agile mind and the rapid-fire questions, which disarmed him somewhat. He sat Canelo in the kitchen, under pans and utensils dangling like a silent audience, with the tap that dripped no matter how tightly it was locked, the forlornness of the women picking flowers in the mural on the wall. *Make me the meal your mother would cook if you were coming home*, Molinari instructed. Canelo made him *tamales* using a corn-based dough, filled with leftover vegetables from the day's menu, meats, cheese, and cooked it wrapped in vine leaves instead of the broad plantain leaves his mother would usually use. It was delicious, big-hearted, warm and earthy. After taking his last bite Molinari asked, *What do the Colombian and the Italian in Vienna have in common? Neither of them knows a Frenchman who can make* tamales *this well*.

And so it was settled. He took Canelo on.

Canelo stood up as abruptly as he'd fallen, grabbing the offending skipping rope, wrapping it, shoving it into the depleted backpack, careful not to take his eyes away from her for long in case she vanished or decided to wander off in the wrong direction. He realised then that maybe she knew the land better than he did. Her aura was calm, her expression relaxed; she smiled patiently at him. He was disconcerted by the combination of innocence and siren he saw in her, by the spool of desire it unlocked in him, from his centre right to his loins in an exchange fraught with vulnerability, carnal longings. He watched her in awe. *Impossible, my God*, he said. Her ears visibly pricked at his mutterings. He discreetly studied the long line of her neck, the positioning of her shoulder blades, the lengthy lashes fanning her cheeks, her back proudly arched, the flare of her buttocks. She smelt like Calandrina bulbs. Short bursts of silver lines flickered under her skin, like lightning in the body. He noticed a cut on her thigh but no blood, beauty born from injury.

Who are you? she asked. *Don't you want to know?*

Surprised by the question, he rocked back on his heels. Grainy particles in his left hiking boot pressed against his toes. *Who am I? I should be asking you that! This was supposed to be a solo excursion. By the way, I can help with that.* He pointed at the cut. He rummaged in the tent, fishing out an old black T-shirt with 'Harlem' in white emblazoned on it, a pair of boxer shorts, longer checked shorts and a belt. He placed a plaster on the cut. He'd already seen her naked so he didn't look away as she slipped the clothes on. He didn't stare either, still aware somewhat of boundaries, though it was hard to maintain those elements from the outside world in a place like this. She sat beside him. They looked into the distance, at the sprinkling of homes far away. They did this quietly for a few moments as if testing whether they could sit in silence together or maybe trying on an awkward new intimacy for size. *I'm Canelo*, he said, looking into golden eyes, watching what was registering.

Canelo, she offered perfectly. Her tongue was so pink it seemed disco-coloured. He watched it dart and settle. He'd never heard his name spoken like that, with a kind of satisfaction and pleasure. It was rebirth on the tongue, plum breaking softly in her mouth.

He worked fourteen-hour days for Molinari, progressing from dishwashing to chopping on the assembly line to cooking. Molinari noticed Canelo had an eye for combining flavour with flair, cleverly updating some of his more rustic dishes, injecting vitality into them, which meant still having the authenticity but presenting a new depth of flavour or subtle twist. Food was ceremonial to Canelo, an act of love both men shared. Molinari wasn't a chef who designated to his team then abandoned the kitchen. He stayed in the trenches with them, barking orders, checking portions, tasting, stepping in if things went wrong, a hulk of a man who moved incredibly well, gesticulating wildly, emoting all over the place and generally being very Italian, which suited Canelo, who'd found a kindred spirit. On some evenings after the restaurant closed, they'd sit together over glasses of Lungarotti Rubesco, two alchemists adding to and subtracting from the menus. And a younger audience came to the restaurant because of Canelo. Word had spread in Vienna. They were curious about the youthful Colombian Molinari had taken under his wing. Who knew revolutions started in kitchens? Molinari shrewdly capitalised on this, and was generous enough to share the limelight, having Canelo meet the customers, investors, reviewers. For two years they worked closely together, with everybody certain the young pretender would inherit the coveted head-chef role, and he was on course to. But one day, he awoke to the sound of the faulty restaurant kitchen tap dripping through his eardrums. For days the sound followed him, unable to fill adequately the crack in him that had bloomed inside mysteriously on chilly Vienna mornings. The drip-drips were tiny rivulets of change he needed to access. The old restlessness came back. One afternoon in the restaurant kitchen, the ancestors' voices assembled into a wind in the doorway. *Nieto, it is time*, they chorused. *This is another man's legacy. You must make way towards your own. A man who does not take any risks cannot know what awaits him, Nieto.* He sensed the air around him change, then a molecular shift occurring inside him. He looked at the mural of flower pickers on the wall. The women had lost their flowers, their eyes gleamed dangerously, their fingers curled in anticipation, as though ready to snatch his tongue from his mouth, a new flower to share, pink and buoyant with language, in their clutches. He broke the heart of Molinari, who, of course, knew deep down he would leave eventually but had ignored it. He gave him his blessing, a vintage bottle of Chianti from Tuscany and an ear to bend whenever he needed it.

He went to Paris. His experience with Molinari meant more doors opened for him. He worked at some of the best restaurants alongside some of the most demanding, revered chefs in high-stakes pressured environments where the kitchens were larger and staff more disposable. Just because you were good at your job didn't mean there weren't ten men lining up behind you. This wasn't the relaxed pace of Vienna but a thriving beast of a city. The French were uncompromising, their palates sophisticated: they demanded perfection. The ancestors' voices temporarily became whispers. He made *coquilles Saint-Jacques, confit de canard*, snapper *en papillote*. He sent money and letters back home, occasionally calling his mother in Bogotá; she had to go to a phone centre in town to speak to him. *I can tell when my son is well and when he is not*, she'd say. *Make sure you give thanks to the ancestors for their guidance. Make sure you move with a humble spirit*, she'd offer, breathing softly, pausing while he took in the cadence of her voice. *A city can crush a man who thinks he knows everything. You must act as if you know nothing. Your father has begun writing notes for you. He says they are not for my eyes. I worry but he consoles me. He still makes the best* arroz de lisa *I ever tasted. The dish that made me marry him.*

Afterwards, he carried the click of the phone with him

into the night, picturing her furrowed brow whenever she asked a loaded question, her dark, elegant hands meant for a woman with a good life in another time, her warm laughter, which gave the feeling of being spontaneous even when you didn't expect it. He tried to mould the distances between them with the sturdy hands he'd inherited from his father, wielding sharp kitchen utensils. Paris meant beautiful women. Canelo dated women from Angola, Liberia, Nigeria, Côte d'Ivoire. Women with skin like cocoa silk on his tongue. He traced the ripples in their backs, like they held delicate revelations, confessed his desires to their puckered nipples while they slept, gathered translucent gems from their belly buttons. He genuinely enjoyed women. He liked their company. He fell in love. He fell out of love. He made mistakes.

Merde! *The kitchen is like a god to you*, a dimple-cheeked lover named Monique once yelled, in the middle of an argument. She'd known the demands of his job from the beginning. He'd placed his hand on her spine as if her heartbeat had migrated there, as if to steady it while it transformed into a trapped nerve signalling the end of their discussion. When things were going well with his lovers, he made them bright plates of food, attempting to get them to identify the secret ingredients.

He rose up the ranks becoming head chef at several restaurants by the time he was thirty. He cooked for statesmen, film stars, government agents and restaurant critics. He made smoked sturgeon, cuts of peppered lamb in a miniature forest with a radish centre; he made delicate, unfurling appetisers on beds of ice, cooked midnight banquets inspired by the photography of Malick Sidibé, the paintings of Salvador Dalí and the architectural feats of Gaudí. He collaborated with an artist, creating the edible body installation in a series of galleries where people ate tiny bites of food off the naked body late into the night, beneath flickering candy-coloured lights to explore the connection between food and carnal desires. He was lauded for his artistry, his inventiveness, the gastronomic experiences he created with such verve, such curiosity, such a sense of wonder. But one day he arrived home to the sound of rubble infiltrating his apartment. He couldn't figure out where it was coming from. He checked the ceilings, secret spaces, pressed his ears against the walls, carefully ran his fingers over them to spot any cracks. The sound of rubble wouldn't leave. It seeped into his chest, crumbling, soon producing a feeling of dissatisfaction in him. He took it as a talisman. He changed direction. He didn't want to be restricted by buildings in urban environments, by what they did to the body and people's sense of connection with each other, or the barriers they imposed. He wanted to cook like his father, where you were at one with the land, the environment and the way it spoke to you, sourcing and championing local ingredients, cooking as an act of love again rather than as performance, as nurture, a way of bringing communities together. He started combining his travels with cooking. The rambling chef was born. *El chef deambulando. Nieto,* the ancestors encouraged, *this is the way! You must always follow the sound that is ahead of you. You must listen to its clever mutations in the air. You must never presume to know it, even when you think you've identified it.*

He cooked for shelter projects, battered women in transition, immigrant communities. He took young people into forests on away-days to teach them the power of food and nature, the beauty of tranquillity, finding your own rhythm away from the pressures of the city. He'd been cooking at a friend's restaurant in Birgu, Malta, when the aneurysm happened. He'd been clutching an oversized aubergine, contemplating how to make it an edible bowl containing a spicy Catalan-inspired soup, when the pain in his head became unbearable and the last flickers of light went dark.

Canelo called the fossil woman Haukena. He loaned her more clothes, fearing they would fray or change in the heat, worried that their environment was conducive to things shifting. They walked around the island together. There was a burning sensation in his chest, dryness in his throat; splinters of heat had become a vanishing trail in his blood. He kept an eye out for any odd cavings in the ground, the sound of another entity caught in the trap, rattling, a creature limping in the path she'd taken to arrive, breathing inconsistently, waiting for an opening, an opportunity to break through from the other side. By the third day, she had a solid grasp of language, arguing with him in ways that were amusing and jarring. *Canelo, you have relatives crying in the lodge,* she said, poking his arm in one instance. *Canelo, the boatman searches for his head in the water. You have to help him find it. Where is your cavity? Let me see. Let me put my tongue there. Canelo, Canelo, Canelo.*

They cooked crabs in the pit together. He was surprised by the ferocity with which she caught them, by the intense look of concentration on her face when they were knee deep in the waters. His phone had died so they danced to music from a small battery-run radio on the shore, to Pavarotti playing, white waters edging towards them, caressing their movements from its watchful proximity.

He spoke to her passionately about food, art, music, astronomy. He talked about desires that remained unspeakable in the world outside, how the pressure to adhere to the rules of that world ground away at the core of you sometimes, a core flickering, like a stray blue flame in the dark. He took a philosophical stance on the nature of work and fulfilment. *What do the symphony conductor and the high-wire walker have in common? They both seek flight. They both want to soar! Does it matter whether one is above ground and one isn't?*

Where is the boatman's cavity? she asked, with a sad

expression as something bobbed in her throat. *Can't you make it right?*

At night, she leaned against his shoulder mimicking a random selection of sounds: a kettle hissing, the whirring of a washing-machine's spin cycle, the tent collapsing. And the discharges from her body, miniature lacunas, glimmered beautifully.

There were two weeks of bliss before things began to wash up on the shore, half scenes and moments from his life: his brain scans crossing the sand, the red paintbrush he'd used to paint the walls of his first apartment, a stash of handwritten recipes his father had left him before he passed, a photograph of his mother, older, smiling sheepishly, standing by a crumbling wall in Bogotá. There was the aubergine he'd been holding when the aneurysm occurred; decayed, tainted by its dance with sickness. A line of frothy water snagged them, tossing them into his eye line before grabbing them again, sucking them into the currents.

He sat in the tent afterwards, sweating profusely and shaking, thinking of the doctor's efficiency in delivering the news, the controlled sympathy, the feeling of helplessness, the air leaving his body, the room morphing into a void where the sound became shrill, the doctor's warning that another rupture could happen.

He lost his sense of taste for a while. A chef who couldn't taste what he was cooking had to become more inventive, clever, mysterious. *El chef deambulando* emerged, cooking through the lands to stir his palate back to life.

He started crying in the tent. He was surrounded by at least ten men with cavities for heads, holding what looked like small pitchforks. He didn't understand how they'd all got in. He closed his eyes as they exited, throwing their pitchforks in an attempt to rescue his items from the currents.

A day later, Haukena got sick. The miniature lacunas from her body turned brown. She stopped eating. Her English became more jumbled, regressing. She wandered the surrounding areas near their spot by herself, as though in transition, singing an ancient Tahitian song, mumbling at the trees, pressing her ears against their trunks, as if absorbing their quiet rhythms to sustain herself. He found her in the pit, tracing the last movements of the animals they had cooked, which had made their way there on list-less evenings. She grabbed the blackened cinders, shoved handfuls of soil into her mouth, rapidly blinking from each swallow, squatting into the pit further. Later, he saw her dry-heaving over the water tanks. Then, in the weathered shell structure with two openings, her body contorted, her arms thrown up to the sky, language completely gone from her tongue.

He awoke the next day to the shuddering of lightning, pale silver lines rippling through the sky, hitting the sand at angles, rampaging across the island scattering sticks, over-turning the table used for chopping, the lodge door flung open. There was a horrible tight feeling in his chest. His limbs ached, as though he'd been on a run while sleeping. He was breathing raggedly. He stumbled out of the tent on instinct.

The fossil was in the air, curling, making that owl sound again. Lightning roared in his eardrums, lightning on sand. His favourite pair of fatigue shorts was strewn on the ground. His brown T-shirt billowed as if catching parts of a shadow. His black Casio watch was abandoned, peeking between two small stones, the glass smashed, the hands still. The fossil cooed. He shook his head. He tried to shake his vision but couldn't. Had there ever been a woman? Had another rupture in his brain come early? Maybe when he was crossing over to the island? Had he simply needed a version of sickness mirrored back at him? Of course Haukena had existed! He'd come inside her, read passages of Volkov to her, danced on the edge of the waters with her, confessed his sins to a nub rising under her skin.

The fossil curled again, surveying the destruction below. Buoyed by the electricity in the air, it took off. The ancestors' voices channelled through, taking root in his eardrums. *Nieto, follow the fossil! What is that sound it is making? You must find out.* He set off after it. The fossil made a sound like a groan, a thud, then a loud cry. He watched it weaving between the trees, following the light, spinning, taunting him, like a trick. He ran, his fingers flexing. He poured every bit of desire to capture what was lost into each movement, his chest breaking open, shocks of pain turning to antennae inside his limbs. His mouth became dry. Thoughts scrambled in his head. Every action seemed inadequate yet necessary. *Nieto*, the ancestors chorused, *to the cliff! It is so beautiful on the precipice.* He chased the fossil up the same cliff he'd been intrigued by in the beginning. He tried to capture the fossil that became a woman: maybe he could disrupt the order of things by actively catching her again. If that was possible. His eyes filled with tears as the fossil became a dune, golden, beautiful, hovering. *Nieto, reach for the sound in the middle*, the ancestors urged. *It is so close.* He flung himself off the top of the cliff into the centre of the dune, screaming euphorically as it refashioned him into an unknown entity within it, shrinking him, stripping him of mass and blood, bone, fluid and sight. And the dune was like a golden nebula speaking in Canelo's childhood voice, floating over the waters, racing towards a dwindling brink.

Acknowledgements

Nudibranch was written during a really difficult period in my life. I'm astonished that this collection came out of that but working on these stories gave me courage, light and kept me going. I have to thank my champions whose belief and faith in me means the world.

A big thank you to my fantastic agent Elise Dillsworth. Thank you for being a brilliant advocate, having my back and those wonderful, warm dinners where we hold the world to rights. We've been through a lot together. I appreciate you immensely. I appreciate the contributions you've made past and present.

Huge thanks to my superb publisher Sharmaine Lovegrove. You are a force of nature. Thank you for your passion, support and energy. For allowing me the space to continue to be myself as an artist and not asking me to compromise on that. Thank you for believing in an experimental, black British voice. It means so much. Keep forging your inspiring path.

Big thanks to the Dialogue team for their efforts: Simon

Osunsade, Millie Seaward, Sophia Schoepfer, Thalia Proctor. Apologies to anyone I've left out.

Big thanks to Ben Okri for seeing something in my writing, being generous enough to want to help elevate it. Big thanks to all the other authors who've given their endorsements. Big thanks to Alex Wheatle, top cornerstone! You are tremendous. I'll never forget how supportive and encouraging you've been during my writing journey.

Thanks to Yvvette Edwards for being a joy, marvellous catch-ups and one of the funniest people I know. Thanks to Bernardine Evaristo for the Hedgebrook residency, which was epic. Thanks to Margaret Busby for New Daughters of Africa. We salute you and the amazing trail you've blazed.

Big thanks to past mentors Donna Daley-Clarke and Gaylene Gould. You helped light a fire under my ass. Thanks to David Kwaw Mensah for being an all around dope dude and confidante. Thanks to Kit Caless for supporting my work and encouraging words. Big thanks to Spread The Word and Words of Colour for the work they do. Thanks to the various supporters and friends along the way. Bookshops, festivals, podcasts, journals, universities, magazines and anthologies that have provided platforms, I appreciate you all.

Amen, Tata, Iredia: what would my world be without you? Big love. Thanks to gloriously complicated, flawed women whose stories I want to keep making visible. Thanks to Mum, I love and admire you always and Dad, you make good trouble. I love you dearly. Thanks for planting the seed on the power of imagination.

Bringing a book from manuscript to what you are reading is a team effort.

Dialogue Books would like to thank everyone at Little, Brown who helped to publish *Nudibranch* in the UK.

Editorial
Sharmaine Lovegrove
Sophia Schoepfer
Thalia Proctor

Contracts
Stephanie Cockburn

Sales
Andrew Cattanach
Viki Cheung
Ben Goddard
Rachael Hum
Hannah Methuen

Publicity
Millie Seaward

Marketing
Emily Moran
Hermione Ireland
Hillary Tisman

Design
Helen Bergh
Duncan Spilling

Production
Narges Nojoumi
Nick Ross
Mike Young

Copy Editor
Hazel Orme

Proof Reader
Sheila McIlwraith